PRAISE FOR

Zero K

"Brilliant and astonishing . . . a masterpiece . . . full of DeLillo's amazing inimitable scalpel perceptions; it's fluent in the ideas we'll be talking about twenty years from now. . . . The effect is transcendent."
—Charles Finch, *Chicago Tribune*

"*Zero K* reminds us of DeLillo's almost Day-Glo powers as a writer and his understanding of the strange, contorted shapes that eternal human concerns (with mortality and time) can take in the new millennium."
—Michiko Kakutani, *The New York Times*

"A mysterious, funny and profound book . . . *Zero K* deserves to win old and new readers alike. It's a marvelous blend of DeLillo's enormous gifts. His bleak humor and edged insight, the alertness and vitality of his prose, the vast, poetic extrapolations are all evident. So is the visceral quickness and wit in the sentences. . . . Extraordinary."
—Sam Lipsyte, *Bookforum*

"Daring . . . provocative . . . exquisite . . . captures the swelling fears of our age." —Ron Charles, *The Washington Post*

More Praise for Zero K

"Zero K grapples with the fact our demise is profoundly at odds with this aspect of us that yearns to exceed every limitation. Circling around this irreconcilable dilemma, DeLillo finds a vital dialogue with his great work *White Noise*. It is this . . . that makes this book a provocative success."

—*San Francisco Chronicle*

"All of Don DeLillo's novels have been death-haunted, but *Zero K* concerns itself with a billionaire and his wife who mean to elude death through cryonics. The novel summons themes and imagery from DeLillo's entire career and brings them to bear on the impossible question of what it might mean to escape time."

—*Vulture*

"Sadness might seem too sincere an emotion to ascribe to a novel written by a postmodernist, but *Zero K* pushes its readers to feel. It is almost impossible to not. With its confluence of screens, strange artwork, empty rooms, long hallways and shaved heads of those soon to be frozen, *Zero K* creates an experiment, and we, its subjects, feel pulled to interact. . . . [*Zero K*], particularly its end, is a slight pivot for the novelist. Yet when a writer is able to capture so many of our anxieties on his pages, a pivot can be profound."

—*The Millions*

"This terrific novel unsettles, disturbs and undermines conventional notions and holds our contemporary existence up for examination."

—*Providence Journal*

"[DeLillo is] the master of the pre-apocalyptic novel, the chief literary mapper of the dehumanized places our current world may lead us. [He] is near the top of his game in *Zero K*."

—*The Dallas Morning News*

"Reveals itself as perhaps the author's most fully animated exploration of human feeling."

—*Vice*

"To reconcile . . . the fear of death that informs so many egregious acts . . . and the little everyday moments that make up so much of life—is the problem DeLillo takes up again and again, and the impossibility of it is what makes his work so powerful, so comical . . . and so fine."

—*Minneapolis Star Tribune*

"DeLillo's prose style has undergone a quickening. His sentences have always had a cascade effect, but lately their arc is steeper. Gravity has assumed more force. And [in *Zero K*] style and theme have something in common."

—*New York* magazine

"Dazzling."

—*St. Louis Post-Dispatch*

"*Zero K* is science fiction of a kind that takes place five minutes from now and a novel of ideas that's deeply emotional."

—*The Seattle Times*

"The novel's brilliance escalates sharply as it proceeds. By the end, it is absolute."

—*The Buffalo News*

"*Zero K* demonstrates the electrifying possibilities of DeLillo's approach. . . . This is speculative fiction in the present tense written with an ardent concentration and economy, no superfluous words, not even a wasted comma. At its best, DeLillo's prose buzzes with the ambient hum of modernity, attuning the reader to a subliminal frequency, the hidden meanings of everyday objects and rituals."

—*Slant Magazine*

"Almost six decades into publishing fiction, this author has put up a fresh career landmark. . . . [DeLillo] has brought off something simple but disturbing, revealing both the perils of faith and the power of Gospel."

—*The Philadelphia Inquirer*

"As ever, DeLillo explores the depths of an edgy, timely topic, completely resisting cliché, and emerges with something both fresh and universal."

—*The Huffington Post*

"There are deep, slicing currents running through *Zero K*, despite its almost ascetic surfaces, and there are unforgettable little moments scattered everywhere in these pages."

—*The Christian Science Monitor*

"In *Zero K*, Don DeLillo has found the perfect physical repository for his oracular visions. . . . His vision is ironic, sere, crackling with static like a horror film."

—*The New York Review of Books*

"Among DeLillo's finest work . . . DeLillo sneaks a heart-breaking story of a son attempting to reconnect with his father into his thought-provoking novel."

—*Publishers Weekly* (starred review)

"Lush in thought and feeling . . . Intently observant and obsessively concerned with language and meaning, Jeffrey is a mesmerizing and disquieting narrator. . . . In this magnificently edgy and profoundly inquisitive tale, DeLillo reflects on what we remember and forget, what we treasure and destroy, and what we fail to do for each other and for life itself. . . . DeLillo reaffirms his standing as one of the world's most significant writers."

—*Booklist* (starred review)

"This is a book that is both beautiful and profound, certainly DeLillo's best since *Underworld*, and will reward repeated reading."

—*The Observer* (UK)

"Haunting . . . Simultaneously terrifying yet beautifully told with a real tenderness for the everyday details of life in New York . . . certainly not to be missed."

—*GQ*

Zero K

A Novel

Don DeLillo

SCRIBNER

New York London Toronto Sydney New Delhi

Scribner
An Imprint of Simon & Schuster, Inc.
1230 Avenue of the Americas
New York, NY 10020

Copyright © 2016 by Don DeLillo

First Scribner trade paperback edition May 2017

SCRIBNER and design are registered trademarks of The Gale Group, Inc., used under license by Simon & Schuster, Inc., the publisher of this work.

For information about special discounts for bulk purchases, please contact Simon & Schuster Special Sales at 1-866-506-1949 or business@simonandschuster.com.

The Simon & Schuster Speakers Bureau can bring authors to your live event. For more information or to book an event, contact the Simon & Schuster Speakers Bureau at 1-866-248-3049 or visit our website at www.simonspeakers.com.

Interior design by Erich Hobbing

Manufactured in the United States of America

1 3 5 7 9 10 8 6 4 2

Library of Congress Control Number: 2015040210

ISBN 978-1-5011-3539-2
ISBN 978-1-5011-3807-2 (pbk)
ISBN 978-1-5011-3540-8 (ebook)

To Barbara

Zero K

PART ONE

In the Time
of Chelyabinsk

- 1 -

Everybody wants to own the end of the world.

    This is what my father said, standing by the contoured windows in his New York office—private wealth management, dynasty trusts, emerging markets. We were sharing a rare point in time, contemplative, and the moment was made complete by his vintage sunglasses, bringing the night indoors. I studied the art in the room, variously abstract, and began to understand that the extended silence following his remark belonged to neither one of us. I thought of his wife, the second, the archaeologist, the one whose mind and failing body would soon begin to drift, on schedule, into the void.

That moment came back to me some months later and half a world away. I sat belted into the rear seat of an armored hatchback with smoked side windows, blind both ways. The driver, partitioned, wore a soccer jersey and sweatpants with a bulge at the hip indicating a sidearm. After an hour's ride over rough roads he brought the car to a stop and said something into his lapel device. Then he eased his head forty-five degrees in the direction of the right rear passenger seat. I took this to mean that it was time for me to unstrap myself and get out.

The ride was the last stage in a marathon journey and I walked away from the vehicle and stood a while, stunned by the heat, holding my overnight bag and feeling my body unwind. I heard the engine start up and turned to watch. The car was headed back to the private airstrip and it was the only thing moving out there, soon to be enveloped in land or sinking light or sheer horizon.

I completed my turn, a long slow scan of salt flats and stone rubble, empty except for several low structures, possibly interconnected, barely separable from the bleached landscape. There was nothing else, nowhere else. I hadn't known the precise nature of my destination, only its remoteness. It was not hard to imagine that my father at his office window had conjured his remark from this same stark terrain and the geometric slabs that blended into it.

He was here now, they both were, father and stepmother, and I'd come to pay the briefest of visits and say an uncertain farewell.

The number of structures was hard to determine from my near vantage. Two, four, seven, nine. Or only one, a central unit with rayed attachments. I imagined it as a city to be discovered at a future time, self-contained, well-preserved, nameless, abandoned by some unknown migratory culture.

The heat made me think I was shrinking but I wanted to remain a moment and look. These were buildings in hiding, agoraphobically sealed. They were blind buildings, hushed and somber, invisibly windowed, designed to fold into themselves, I thought, when the movie reaches the point of digital collapse.

I followed a stone path to a broad portal where two men stood watching. Different soccer jerseys, same hip bulge. They stood behind a set of bollards designed to keep vehicles from entering the immediate area.

Off to the side, at the far edge of the entranceway, strangely, two other figures, in chadors, shrouded women standing motionless.

- 2 -

My father had grown a beard. This surprised me. It was slightly grayer than the hair on his head and had the effect of setting off his eyes, intensifying the gaze. Was this the beard a man grows who is eager to enter a new dimension of belief?

I said, "When does it happen?"

"We're working on the day, the hour, the minute. Soon," he said.

He was in his mid-to-late sixties, Ross Lockhart, broad-shouldered and agile. His dark glasses sat on the desk in front of him. I was accustomed to meeting him in offices, somewhere or other. This one was improvised, several screens, keyboards and other devices set about the room. I was aware that he'd put major sums of money into this entire operation, this endeavor, called the Convergence, and the office was a gesture of courtesy, allowing him to maintain convenient contact with his network of companies, agencies, funds, trusts, foundations, syndicates, communes and clans.

"And Artis."

"She's completely ready. There's no trace of hesitation or second thoughts."

"We're not talking about spiritual life everlasting. This is the body."

"The body will be frozen. Cryonic suspension," he said.

"Then at some future time."

"Yes. The time will come when there are ways to counteract the circumstances that led to the end. Mind and body are restored, returned to life."

"This is not a new idea. Am I right?"

"This is not a new idea. It is an idea," he said, "that is now approaching full realization."

I was disoriented. This was the morning of what would be my first full day here and this was my father across the desk and none of it was familiar, not the situation or the physical environment or the bearded man himself. I'd be on my way home before I'd be able to absorb any of it.

"And you have complete confidence in this project."

"Complete. Medically, technologically, philosophically."

"People enroll their pets," I said.

"Not here. Nothing here is speculative. Nothing is wishful or peripheral. Men, women. Death, life."

His voice carried the even tone of a challenge.

"Is it possible for me to see the area where it happens?"

"Extremely doubtful," he said.

Artis, his wife, was suffering from several disabling illnesses. I knew that multiple sclerosis was largely responsible for her deterioration. My father was here as devoted witness to her passing and then as educated observer of whatever initial methods would allow preservation of the body until the year, the decade, the day when it might safely be permitted to reawaken.

"When I got here I was met by two armed escorts. Took me through security, took me to the room, said next to nothing. That's all I know. And the name, which sounds religious."

"Faith-based technology. That's what it is. Another god. Not so different, it turns out, from some of the earlier ones. Except that it's real, it's true, it delivers."

"Life after death."

"Eventually, yes."

"The Convergence."

"Yes."

"There's a meaning in mathematics."

"There's a meaning in biology. There's a meaning in physiology. Let it rest," he said.

When my mother died, at home, I was seated next to the bed and there was a friend of hers, a woman with a cane, standing in the doorway. That's how I would picture the moment, narrowed, now and always, to the woman in the bed, the woman in the doorway, the bed itself, the metal cane.

Ross said, "Down in an area that serves as a hospice I sometimes stand among the people being prepared to undergo the process. Anticipation and awe intermingled. Far more palpable than apprehension or uncertainty. There's a reverence, a state of astonishment. They're together in this. Something far larger than they'd ever imagined. They feel a common mission, a destination. And I find myself trying to imagine such a place centuries back. A lodging, a shelter for travelers. For pilgrims."

"Okay, pilgrims. We're back to the old-time religion. Is it possible for me to visit the hospice?"

"Probably not," he said.

He gave me a small flat disk appended to a wristband. He said it was similar to the ankle monitor that kept police agencies informed of a suspect's whereabouts, pending trial. I'd be allowed entry to certain areas on this level and the one above, nowhere else. I could not remove the wristband without alerting security.

"Don't be quick to draw conclusions about what you see and hear. This place was designed by serious people. Respect the idea. Respect the setting itself. Artis says we ought to regard it as a work-in-progress, an earthwork, a form of earth art, land art. Built up out of the land and sunk down into it as well. Restricted access. Defined by stillness, both human and environmental. A little tomblike as well. The earth is the guiding principle," he said. "Return to the earth, emerge from the earth."

I spent time walking the halls. The halls were nearly empty, three people, at intervals, and I nodded to each, receiving only a single grudging glance. The walls were shades of green. Down one broad hall, turn into another. Blank walls, no windows, doors widely spaced, all doors shut. These were doors of related colors, subdued, and I wondered if there was meaning to be found in these slivers of the spectrum. This is what I did in any new environment. I tried to inject meaning, make the place coherent or at least locate myself within the place, to confirm my uneasy presence.

At the end of the last hall there was a screen jutting from a niche in the ceiling. It began to lower, stretching wall to wall and reaching nearly to the floor. I approached slowly. At first the images were all water. There was water racing through woodlands and surging over riverbanks. There were scenes of rain beating on terraced fields, long moments of nothing but rain, then people everywhere running, others helpless in small boats bouncing over rapids. There were temples flooded, homes pitching down hillsides. I watched as water kept rising in city streets, cars and drivers going under. The size of the screen lifted the effect out of the category of TV news. Everything loomed, scenes lasted long past the usual broadcast breath. It was there in front of me, on my level, immediate and real, a woman sitting life-sized on a lopsided chair in a house collapsed in mudslide. A man, a face, underwater, staring out at me. I had to step back but also had to keep looking. It was hard not to look. Finally I glanced back down the hall waiting for someone to appear, another witness, a person who might stand next to me while the images built and clung.

There was no audio.

- 3 -

Artis was alone in the suite where she and Ross were staying. She sat in an armchair, wearing robe and slippers, and
appeared to be asleep.

What do I say? How do I begin?

You look beautiful, I thought, and she did, sadly so, attenuated by illness, lean face and ash-blond hair, uncombed,
pale hands folded in her lap. I used to think of her as the
Second Wife and then as the Stepmother and then, again,
as the Archaeologist. This last product label was not so
reductive, mainly because I was finally getting to know her.
I liked to imagine that she was the scientist as ascetic, living for periods in crude encampments, someone who might
readily adapt to unsparing conditions of another kind.

Why did my father ask me to come here?

He wanted me to be with him when Artis died.

I sat on a cushioned bench, watching and waiting, and
soon my thoughts fell away from the still figure in the chair
and then there he was, there we were, Ross and I, in minia-
turized mindspace.

He was a man shaped by money. He'd made an early reputation by analyzing the profit impact of natural disasters. He liked to talk to me about money. My mother said, What about sex, that's what he needs to know. The language of money was complicated. He defined terms, drew diagrams, seemed to be living in a state of emergency, planted in the office most days for ten or twelve hours, or rushing to airports, or preparing for conferences. At home he stood before a full-length mirror reciting from memory speeches he was working on about risk appetites and offshore jurisdictions, refining his gestures and facial expressions. He had an affair with an office temp. He ran in the Boston Marathon.

What did I do? I mumbled, I shuffled, I shaved a strip of hair along the middle of my head, front to back—I was his personal antichrist.

He left when I was thirteen. I was doing my trigonometry homework when he told me. He sat across the small desk where my ever-sharpened pencils jutted from an old marmalade jar. I kept doing my homework while he spoke. I examined the formulas on the page and wrote in my notebook, over and over: *sine cosine tangent*.

Why did my father leave my mother?

Neither ever said.

Years later I lived in a room-and-a-half rental in upper Manhattan. One evening there was my father on TV, an obscure channel, poor reception, Ross in Geneva, sort of double-imaged, speaking French. Did I know that my father spoke French? Was I sure that this man was my father? He made a reference, in subtitles, to the ecology of unemployment. I watched standing up.

And Artis now in this barely believable place, this desert

apparition, soon to be preserved, a glacial body in a massive burial chamber. And after that a future beyond imagining. Consider the words alone. *Time, fate, chance, immortality.* And here is my simpleminded past, my dimpled history, the moments I can't help summoning because they're mine, impossible not to see and feel, crawling out of every wall around me.

Ash Wednesday, once, I went to church and stood in line. I looked around at the statues, plaques and pillars, the stained glass windows, and then I went to the altar rail and knelt. The priest approached and made his mark, a splotch of holy ash thumb-printed to my forehead. *Dust thou art.* I was not Catholic, my parents were not Catholic. I didn't know what we were. We were Eat and Sleep. We were Take Daddy's Suit to the Dry Cleaner.

When he left I decided to embrace the idea of being abandoned, or semi-abandoned. My mother and I understood and trusted each other. We went to live in Queens, in a garden apartment that had no garden. This suited us both. I let the hair grow back on my aboriginal shaved head. We went for walks together. Who does this, mother and teenage son, in the United States of America? She did not lecture me, or rarely did, on my swerves out of observable normality. We ate bland food and batted a tennis ball back and forth on a public court.

But the robed priest and the small grinding action of his thumb implanting the ash. *And to dust thou shalt return.* I walked the streets looking for people who might look at me. I stood in front of store windows studying my reflection. I didn't know what this was. Was this some freakified gesture of reverence? Was I playing a trick on Holy Mother Church? Or was I simply attempting to thrust myself into meaningful sight? I wanted the stain to last for days and weeks. When I got home my mother leaned back away from me as if to gain perspective. It was the briefest of appraisals. I made it a point not to grin—I had a gravedigger's grin. She said something about the boring state of Wednesdays throughout the world. A little ash, at minimum expense, and a Wednesday, here and there, she said, becomes something to remember.

Eventually my father and I began to jostle our way through some of the tensions that had kept us at a distance and I accepted certain arrangements he made concerning my education but went nowhere near the businesses he owned.

And years later, it felt like a lifetime later, I began to know the woman who now sat before me, leaning into the light shed by a table lamp nearby.

And in another lifetime, hers, she opened her eyes and saw me sitting there.

"Jeffrey."

"Arrived late yesterday."

"Ross told me."

"And it turns out to be true."

I took her hand and held it. There seemed to be nothing more to say but we spoke for an hour. Her voice was a near whisper and so was mine, in accord with the circumstances, or the environment itself, the long hushed hallways, the sense of enclosure and isolation, a new generation of earth art, with human bodies in states of suspended animation.

"Since coming here I've found myself concentrating on small things, then smaller. My mind is unwinding, unspooling. I think of details buried for years. I see moments that I missed before or thought too trivial to recall. It's my condition, of course, or my medication. It's a sense of closing down, coming to an end."

"Temporarily."

"Do you have trouble believing this? Because I don't. I've studied the matter," she said.

"I know you have."

"Skepticism of course. We need this. But at a certain point we begin to understand there's something so much larger and more enduring."

"Here's a simple question. Practical, not skeptical. Why aren't you in the hospice?"

"Ross wants me nearby. Doctors visit regularly."

She had trouble dealing with the congested syllables in this last word and spoke more slowly from this point on.

"Or I get wheeled along corridors and into dark enclosures that move up and down in a shaft or maybe sideways or backwards. In any case I'm taken to an examining room where they watch and listen, all so silently. There's a nurse somewhere in this suite, or nurses. We speak Mandarin, she and I, or he and I."

"Do you think about the kind of world you'll be returning to?"

"I think about drops of water."

I waited.

She said, "I think about drops of water. How I used to stand in the shower and watch a drop of water edge down the inside of the sheer curtain. How I concentrated on the drop, the droplet, the orblet, and waited for it to assume new shapes as it passed across ridges and folds, with water pounding against the side of my head. I remember this from when? Twenty years ago, thirty, longer? I don't know. What was I thinking at the time? I don't know. Maybe I gave a certain kind of life to the drop of water. I animated it, cartooned it. I don't know. Probably my mind was mostly blank. The water that's smacking my head is damn cold but I don't bother adjusting the flow. I need to watch the drop, see it begin to lengthen, to ooze. But it's too clear and transparent to be a thing that oozes. I stand there getting smacked in the head while I tell myself there is no oozing. Ooze is mud or slime, it's primitive life at the ocean bottom and it's made chiefly of microscopic sea creatures."

She spoke a kind of shadow language, pausing, thinking, trying to remember, and when she came back to this moment, this room, she had to place me, re-situate me, Jeffrey, son of, seated across from her. I was Jeff to everyone but Artis. That extra syllable, in her tender voice, made me self-aware, or aware of a second self, more agreeable and dependable, a man who walks with his shoulders squared, pure fiction.

"Sometimes in a dark room," I said, "I will shut my eyes. I walk into the room and shut my eyes. Or, in the bedroom, I wait until I approach the lamp that sits on the bureau next to the bed. Then I shut my eyes. Is this a surrender to the dark? I don't know what this is. Is this an accommodation? Let the dark dictate the terms of the situation? What is this? Sounds like something a weird kid does. The kid I used to be. But I do it even now. I walk into a dark room and maybe wait a moment and stand in the doorway and then shut my eyes. Am I testing myself by doubling the dark?"

We were quiet for a time.

"Things we do and then forget about," she said.

"Except that we don't forget. People like us."

I liked saying that. People like us.

"One of those small divots of personality. This is what Ross says. He says that I'm a foreign country. Small things, then smaller. This has become my state of being."

"I make my way toward the bureau in the dark bedroom and try to sense the location of the table lamp and then feel or grope for the lampshade and reach under the lampshade for the on-off thing, the knob, the switch that will turn on the light."

"Then you open your eyes."

"Or do I? The weird kid might keep them closed."

"But only on Mondays, Wednesdays and Fridays," she said, barely managing to make her way through the familiar strand of days.

Someone came out of a back room, a woman, gray jumpsuit, dark hair, dark face, businesslike expression. She wore latex gloves and stood in position behind Artis, looking at me.

Time to leave.

Artis said weakly, "It is only me, the body in the shower, one person enclosed in plastic watching a drop of water skate down the wet curtain. The moment is there to be forgotten. This seems the ultimate point. It's a moment never to be thought of except when it's in the process of unfolding. Maybe this is why it doesn't seem peculiar. It is only me. I don't think about it. I simply live within it and then leave it behind. But not forever. Leave it behind except for now, in this particular place, where everything I've ever said and done and thought about is near to hand, right here, to be gathered tightly so it doesn't disappear when I open my eyes to the second life."

It was called a food unit and this is what it was, a component, a module, four undersized tables and one other person, a man who wore what appeared to be a monk's cloak. I ate and watched, using stealth glances. He cut his food and chewed it, introspectively. When he stood up to leave, I saw faded blue jeans below the cloak and tennis shoes below the jeans. The food was edible but not always nameable.

I entered my room by placing the disk on my wristband against the magnetic fixture embedded in the middle panel of the door. The room was small and featureless. It was generic to the point of being a thing with walls. The ceiling was low, the bed was bedlike, the chair was a chair. There were no windows.

In twenty-four hours, based on the clinical estimate, Artis would be dead, which meant that I would be on my way home while Ross remained for a time to determine firsthand that the series of cryonic actions was proceeding on schedule.

But I was already feeling trapped. Visitors were not permitted to leave the building and even with nowhere to go out there, among those Precambrian rocks, I felt the effects of this restriction. The room was not equipped with digital connections and my smartphone was brain-dead here. I did stretching exercises to get the blood pumping. I did sit-ups and squat-jumps. I tried to remember the dream of the previous night.

The room made me feel that I was being absorbed into the essential content of the place. I sat in the chair, eyes closed. I saw myself sitting here. I saw the complex itself from somewhere in the stratosphere, solid welded mass and variously pitched roofs, sun-struck walls.

I saw the drops of water that Artis had watched, one by one, trickling down the inside of the shower curtain.

I saw Artis vaguely naked, facing into the spray of water, the image of her eyes closed within the fact of my eyes closed.

I wanted to get out of the chair, walk out of the room, say goodbye to her and leave. I managed to talk myself up to a standing position and then open the door. But all I did was walk the halls.

- 4 -

I walked the halls. The doors here were painted in gradations of muted blue and I tried to name the shades. Sea, sky, butterfly, indigo. All these were wrong and I began to feel more foolish with every step I took and every door I scrutinized. I wanted to see a door open and a person emerge. I wanted to know where I was and what was happening around me. A woman came striding by, briskly, and I resisted an impulse to name her like a color, or examine her for signs of something, clues to something.

Then the idea hit me. Simple. There was nothing behind the doors. I walked and thought. I speculated. There were areas on certain floors that contained offices. Elsewhere the halls were pure design, the doors simply one element in the overarching scheme, which Ross had described in a general way. I wondered whether this was visionary art, involving colors, forms and local materials, art meant to accompany and surround the hardwired initiative, the core work of scientists, counselors, technicians and medical personnel.

I liked the idea. It fit the circumstances, it met the standards of unlikelihood, or daring dumb luck, that can mark the most compelling art. All I had to do was knock on a door. Pick a color, pick a door and knock. If no one opens the door, knock on the next door and the next. But I was wary of betraying my father's trust in bringing me here. Then there were the hidden cameras. There would have to be surveillance of these hallways, with blank faces in hushed rooms scanning the monitors.

Three people came toward me, one of them a boy in a motorized wheelchair that resembled a toilet. He was nine or ten and watched me all the way. His upper body was tilted severely to one side but his eyes were alert and I wanted to stop and talk to him. The adults made it clear that this was not possible. They flanked the wheelchair and stared straight ahead, into authorized space, stranding me in my pause, my good intentions.

Soon I was turning a corner and going down a hall with walls painted raw umber, a thick runny pigment meant to resemble mud, I thought. There were matching doors, all doors the same. There was also a recess in the wall and a figure standing there, arms, legs, head, torso, a thing fixed in place. I saw that it was a mannequin, naked, hairless, without facial features, and it was reddish brown, maybe russet or simply rust. There were breasts, it had breasts, and I stopped to study the figure, a molded plastic version of the human body, a jointed model of a woman. I imagined placing a hand on a breast. This seemed required, particularly if you are me. The head was a near oval, arms positioned in a manner that I tried to decipher—self-defense, withdrawal, with one foot set to the rear. The figure was rooted to the floor, not enclosed in protective glass. A hand on a breast, a hand sliding up a thigh. It's something I would have done once upon a time. Here and now, the cameras in place, the monitors, an alarm mechanism on the body itself—I was sure of this. I stood back and looked. The stillness of the figure, the empty face, the empty hallway, the figure at night, a dummy, in fear, drawing away. I moved farther back and kept on looking.

Finally I decided that I had to find out whether there was anything behind the doors. I dismissed the possible consequences. I walked down the hall, chose a door and knocked. I waited, went to the next door and knocked. Waited, went to the next door and knocked. I did this six times and told myself one more door and this time the door opened and a man stood there in suit, tie and turban. I looked at him, considering what I might say.

"I must have the wrong door," I said.

He gave me a hard look.

"They're all the wrong door," he said.

It took me a while to find my father's office.

Once, when they were still married, my father called my mother a fishwife. This may have been a joke but it sent me to the dictionary to look up the word. Coarse woman, a shrew. I had to look up *shrew*. A scold, a nag, from Old English for shrewmouse. I had to look up *shrewmouse*. The book sent me back to *shrew*, sense 1. A small insectivorous mammal. I had to look up *insectivorous*. The book said it meant feeding on insects, from Latin *insectus*, for insect, plus Latin *vora*, for vorous. I had to look up *vorous*.

Three or four years later I was trying to read a lengthy and intense European novel, written in the 1930s, translated from the German, and I came across the word *fishwife*. It swept me back into the marriage. But when I tried to imagine their life together, mother and father minus me, I came up with nothing, I knew nothing. Ross and Madeline alone, what did they say, what were they like, who were they? All I felt was a shattered space where my father used to be. And here was my mother, sitting across a room, a thin woman in trousers and a gray shirt. When she asked me about the book, I made a gesture of helplessness. The book was a challenge, a secondhand paperback crammed with huge and violent emotions in small crowded type on waterlogged pages. She told me to put it down and pick it up again in three years. But I wanted to read it now, I needed it now, even if I knew I'd never finish. I liked reading books that nearly killed me, books that helped tell me who I was, the son who spites his father by reading such books. I liked sitting on our tiny concrete balcony, reading, with a fractional view of the ring of glass and steel where my father worked, amid lower Manhattan's bridges and towers.

When Ross was not seated behind a desk, he was standing by a window. But there were no windows in this office.

I said, "And Artis."

"Being examined. Soon to be medicated. She spends time, necessarily, in a medicated state. She calls it languid contentment."

"I like that."

He repeated the phrase. He liked it too. He was in shirt-sleeves, wearing his dark glasses, nostalgically called KGBs—polarized, with swoop lenses and variable tint.

"We had a talk, she and I."

"She told me. You'll see her again, talk again. Tomorrow," he said.

"In the meantime. This place."

"What about it?"

"I knew only what little you told me. I was traveling blind. First the car and driver, then the company plane, Boston to New York."

"Super-midsize jet."

"Two men came aboard. Then New York to London."

"Colleagues."

"Who said nothing to me. Not that I minded."

"And who got off at Gatwick."

"I thought it was Heathrow."

"It was Gatwick," he said.

"Then somebody came aboard and took my passport and brought it back and we were airborne again. I was alone in the cabin. I think I slept. I ate something, I slept, then we landed. I never saw the pilot. I was guessing Frankfurt. Somebody came aboard, took my passport, brought it back. I checked the stamp."

"Zurich," he said.

"Then three people boarded, man, two women. The older woman smiled at me. I tried to hear what they were saying."

"They were speaking Portuguese."

He was enjoying this, straight-faced, slumped in the chair, his remarks directed toward the ceiling.

"They talked but did not eat. I had a snack, or maybe that was later, in the next stage. We landed and they got off and somebody came aboard and led me onto the tarmac to another plane. He was a baldheaded guy about seven feet tall wearing a dark suit and a large silver medallion on a chain around his neck."

"You were in Minsk."

"Minsk," I said.

"Which is in Belarus."

"I don't think anybody stamped my passport. The plane was different from the original."

"Rusjet charter."

"Smaller, fewer amenities, no other passengers. Belarus," I said.

"You flew southeast from there."

"I was drowsy, stupefied, half-dead. I'm not sure whether the next stage was stop or nonstop. I'm not sure how many stages in the entire trip. I slept, dreamt, hallucinated."

"What were you doing in Boston?"

"My girlfriend lives there."

"You and your girlfriends never seem to live in the same city. Why is that?"

"It makes time more precious."

"Very different here," he said.

"I know. I've learned this. There is no time."

"Or time is so overwhelming that we don't feel it pass in the same way."

"You hide from it."

"We defer to it," he said.

It was my turn to slump in the chair. I wanted a cigarette. I'd stopped smoking twice and wanted to start and stop again. I envisioned it as a lifelong cycle.

"Do I ask the question or do I accept the situation passively? I want to know the rules."

"What's the question?"

"Where are we?" I said.

He nodded slowly, examining the matter. Then he laughed.

"The nearest city of any size is across the border, called Bishkek. It's the capital of Kyrgyzstan. Then there's Almaty, bigger, more distant, in Kazakhstan. But Almaty is not the capital. It used to be the capital. The capital is now Astana, which has gold skyscrapers and indoor shopping malls where people lounge on sand beaches before plunging into wave pools. Once you know the local names and how to spell them, you'll feel less detached."

"I won't be here that long."

"True," he said. "But there's a change in the estimate concerning Artis. They expect it to happen one day later."

"I thought the timing was extremely precise."

"You don't have to stay. She'll understand."

"I'll stay. Of course I'll stay."

"Even under the most detailed guidance, the body tends to influence certain decisions."

"Is she dying naturally or is the last breath being induced?"

"You understand there's something beyond the last breath. You understand this is only the preface to something larger, to what is next."

"It seems very businesslike."

"It will be very gentle in fact."

"Gentle."

"It will be quick, safe and painless."

"Safe," I said.

"They need it to happen in complete synchronization with the methods they've been fine-tuning. Best suited to her body, her illness. She could live weeks longer, yes, but to what end?"

He was leaning forward now, elbows on the desk.

I said, "Why here?"

"There are laboratories and tech centers in two other countries. This is the base, central command."

"But why so isolated? Why not Switzerland? Why not a suburb of Houston?"

"This is what we want, this separation. We have what is needed. Durable energy sources and strong mechanized systems. Blast walls and fortified floors. Structural redundancy. Fire safety. Security patrols, land and air. Elaborate cyberdefense. And so on."

Structural redundancy. He liked saying that. He opened a drawer in the desk, then held up a bottle of Irish whiskey. He pointed to a tray that held two glasses and I went across the room to get it. Back at the desk I inspected the glasses, looking for infiltrations of sand and grit.

"People in offices here. Hidden away. What are they doing?"

"They're making the future. A new idea of the future. Different from the others."

"And it has to be here."

"This is land traveled by nomads for thousands of years. Sheepherders in open country. It's not battered and compacted by history. History is buried here. Thirty years ago

Artis worked on a dig somewhere north and east of here, near China. History in burial mounds. We're outside the limits. We're forgetting everything we knew."

"You can forget your name in this place."

He raised his glass and drank. The whiskey was a rare blend, triple distilled, production strictly limited. He'd given me the details years ago.

"What about the money?"

"Whose?"

"Yours. You're in big, obviously."

"I used to think I was a serious man. The work I did, the effort and dedication. Then, later, the time I was able to devote to other matters, to art, educating myself to the ideas and traditions and innovations. Came to love it," he said. "The work itself, a picture on a wall. Then I got started on rare books. Spent hours and days in libraries, in restricted areas, and it wasn't a need for acquisition."

"You had access denied to others."

"But I wasn't there to acquire. I was there to stand and look, or squat and look. To read the titles on the spines of priceless books in the caged stacks. Artis and I. You and I, once, in New York."

I felt the smooth burn of the whiskey going down and closed my eyes for a moment, listening to Ross reciting titles he recalled from libraries in several world capitals.

"But what's more serious than money?" I said. "What's the term? Exposure. What's your exposure in this project?"

I spoke without an edge. I said these things quietly, without irony.

"Once I was educated to the significance of the idea, and the potential behind it, the enormous implications," he said, "I made a decision that I've never second-guessed."

"Have you ever second-guessed anything?"

"My first marriage," he said.

I stared into my glass.

"And who was she?"

"Good question. Profound question. We had a son but other than that."

I didn't want to look at him.

"But who was she?"

"She was essentially one thing. She was your mother."

"Say her name."

"Did we ever say each other's name, she and I?"

"Say her name."

"People who are married to each other as we were, in our uncommon way, which is not so uncommon, do they ever say each other's name?"

"Just once. I need to hear you say it."

"We had a son. We said his name."

"Indulge me. Go ahead. Say it."

"Do you remember what you said a minute ago? You can forget your name in this place. People lose their names in a number of ways."

"Madeline," I said. "My mother, Madeline."

"Now I remember, yes."

He smiled and settled back in an attitude of fake reminiscence, then changed expression, a well-timed maneuver, addressing me sharply.

"Think about this, what is here and who is here. Think about the end of all the petty misery you've been hoarding for years. Think beyond personal experience. Leave it back there. What's happening in this community is not just a creation of medical science. There are social theorists involved, and biologists, and futurists, and geneticists, and climatologists, and neuroscientists, and psychologists, and ethicists, if that's the right word."

"Where are they?"

"Some are here permanently, others come and go. There are the numbered levels. All the vital minds. Global English, yes, but other languages as well. Translators when necessary, human and electronic. There are philologists designing an advanced language unique to the Convergence. Word roots, inflections, even gestures. People will learn it and speak it. A language that will enable us to express things we can't express now, see things we can't see now, see ourselves and others in ways that unite us, broaden every possibility."

He tossed down another dram or two, then held the glass under his nose and sniffed. It was empty, for now.

"We fully expect that this site we occupy will eventually become the heart of a new metropolis, maybe an independent state, different from any we've known. This is what I mean when I call myself a serious man."

"With serious money."

"Yes, money."

"Tons of it."

"And other benefactors. Individuals, foundations, corporations, secret funding from various governments by way of their intelligence agencies. This idea is a revelation to smart people in many disciplines. They understand that now is the time. Not just the science and technology but political and even military strategies. Another way to think and live."

He poured carefully, an amount he liked to call a finger-breadth. His glass, then mine.

"First for Artis, of course. For the woman she is, for what she means to me. Then the leap into total acceptance. The conviction, the principle."

Think of it this way, he told me. Think of your life span measured in years and then measured in seconds. Years, eighty years. Sounds okay by current standards. And then seconds, he said. Your life in seconds. What's the equivalent of eighty years?

He paused, maybe running the numbers. Seconds, minutes, hours, days, weeks, months, years, decades.

Seconds, he said. Start counting. Your life in seconds. Think of the age of the earth, the geologic eras, oceans appearing and disappearing. Think of the age of the galaxy, the age of the universe. All those billions of years. And us, you and me. We live and die in a flash.

Seconds, he said. We can measure our time in seconds.

He wore a blue dress shirt, no tie, top two buttons undone. I played with the idea that the shirt's color matched one of the hall doors of my recent experience. Maybe I was trying to undermine the discourse, a form of self-defense.

He took off his glasses and set them down. He looked tired, he looked older. I watched him drink and then pour and I waved off the thrust bottle.

I said, "If someone had told me all this, weeks ago, this

place, these ideas, someone I trust completely, I guess I would have believed it. But I'm here, and it's all around me, and I have trouble believing it."

"You need a good night's sleep."

"Bishkek. Is that it?"

"And Almaty. But at a considerable distance, both. And to the north somewhere, way up, far up, that's where the Soviets tested their nuclear bombs."

We thought about this.

"You have to get beyond your experience," he said. "Beyond your limitations."

"I need a window to look out of. That's my limitation."

He raised his glass and waited for me to match the gesture.

"I took you to the playground, that old ruin of a playground where we were living then. I put you on the swing and I pushed and waited and pushed," he said. "The swing flew out, the swing came back. I put you on the seesaw. I stood on the other side of the balancing bar and pushed down slowly on my end of the plank. You went up in the air, your hands fastened to the grip. Then I raised the plank at my end and watched you drop down. Up and down. A little faster now. Up and down, up and down. I made sure you held tight to the handgrip. I said, *See-saw, see-saw.*"

I paused a moment and then raised my glass, waiting for whatever was next.

I stood before the screen in the long hallway. Nothing but sky at first, then an intimation of threat, treetops leaning, unnatural light. Soon, in seconds, a rotating column of wind, dirt and debris. It began to fill the frame, a staggered funnel, dark and bent, soundless, and then another, down left, in the far distance, rising from the horizon line. This was flat land, view unobstructed, the screen all tornado now, an awed silence that I thought would break into open roar.

Here was our climate enfolding us. I'd seen many tornadoes on TV news reports and waited for the footage of the rubbled storm path, the aftermath, houses in a shattered line, roofs blown off, siding in collapse.

It appeared, yes, whole streets leveled, school bus on its side, but also people coming this way, in slow motion, nearly out of the screen and into the hall, carrying what they'd salvaged, a troop of men and women, black and white, in solemn march, and the dead arrayed on ravaged floorboards in front yards. The camera lingered on the bodies. The detailwork of their violent end was hard to watch. But I watched, feeling obligated to something or someone, the victims perhaps, and thinking of myself as lone witness, sworn to the task.

Now, somewhere else, another town, another time of day, a young woman on a bicycle pedaling past, foreground, oddly comic motion, quick and jittery, one end of the screen to the other, with a mile-wide storm, a vortex, still far off, crawling up out of the seam of earth and sky, and then cut to an obese man lurching down basement steps, ultra-real, families huddled in garages, faces in the dark, and the girl on the bike again, pedaling the other way now, carefree, without urgency, a scene in an old silent movie, she is Buster Keaton in nitwit innocence, and then a reddish flash of light and the thing was right here, touching down massively, sucking up half a house, pure power, truck and barn squarely in the path.

White screen, while I stood waiting.

Total wasteland now, a sheared landscape, the image persisting, the silence as well. I stood in place for some minutes, waiting, houses gone, girl on bike gone, nothing, finished, done. The same drained screen.

I continued to wait, expecting more. I felt a whiskey belch erupting from some deep sac. There was nowhere to go and I had no idea what time it was. My watch was fixed on North American time, eastern standard.

- 5 -

I'd seen him once before, here in the food unit, the man in the monk's cloak. He did not look up when I entered. A meal appeared in a slot near the door and I took the plate, glass and utensils to a table positioned diagonally to his, across a narrow aisle.

He had a long face and large hands, head narrowing toward the top, hair cropped to the skull, leaving sparse gray stubble. The cloak was the same one he'd been wearing last time, old and wrinkled, purplish, with gold embellishments. It had no sleeves. What emerged from the cloak were pajama sleeves, striped.

I examined the food, took a bite and decided to assume that he spoke English.

"What is this we're eating?"

He looked over at my plate, although not at me.

"It's called morning *plov*."

I took another bite and tried to associate the taste with the name.

"Can you tell me what that is?"

"Carrots and onions, some mutton, some rice."

"I see the rice."

"*Oshi nahor,*" he said.

We ate quietly for a time.

"What do you do here?"

"I talk to the dying."

"You reassure them."

"What do I reassure them of?"

"The continuation. The reawakening."

"Do you believe that?"

"Don't you?" I said.

"I don't think I want to. I just talk about the end. Calmly, quietly."

"But the idea itself. The reason behind this entire venture. You don't accept it."

"I want to die and be finished forever. Don't you want to die?" he said.

"I don't know."

"What's the point of living if we don't die at the end of it?"

In his voice I tried to detect origins in some secluded bend of the English language, pitch and tone possibly hedged by time, tradition and other languages.

"What brought you here?"

He had to think about this.

"Maybe something someone said. I just drifted in. I was living in Tashkent during the unrest. Many hundreds dead all through the country. They boil people to death there. The medieval mind. I tend to enter countries in their periods of violent unrest. I was learning to speak Uzbek and helping educate the children of one of the provincial officials. I taught them English word by word and tried to minister to the man's wife, who had been ill for several years. I performed the functions of a cleric."

He took some food, chewed and swallowed. I did the same and waited for him to continue. The food was beginning to taste like what it was, now that he'd identified it for me. Mutton. Morning *plov*. It seemed he had nothing further to say.

"And are you a cleric?"

"I was a member of a post-evangelist group. We were radical breakaways from the world council. We had chapters in seven countries. The number kept changing. Five, seven, four, eight. We met in simple structures that we built ourselves. Mastabas. Inspired by tombs in very ancient Egypt."

"Mastabas."

"Flat roof, sloped walls, rectangular base."

"You met in tombs."

"We were fiercely awaiting the year, the day, the moment."

"Something would happen."

"What would it be? A meteoroid, a solid mass of stone or metal. An asteroid falling from space, two hundred kilometers in diameter. We knew the astrophysics. An object striking the earth."

"You wanted it to happen."

"We lusted after it. We prayed for it incessantly. It would come from out there, the great expanse of the galaxies, the infinite reach that contains every particle of matter. All the mysteries."

"Then it happened."

"Things fall into the ocean. Satellites falling out of orbit, space probes, space debris, pieces of space junk, man-made. Always the ocean," he said. "Then it happened. A thing hits skimmingly."

"Chelyabinsk," I said.

He let the name dangle. The name itself was a justification. Such events really happen. Those who devote themselves to the occurrence of such events, whatever the scale, whatever the damage, are not dealing in make-believe.

He said, "Siberia was put there to catch these things."

I understood that he did not see the person he was talking to. He had the drifter's inclination to be impervious to names and faces. These were interchangeable components room to room, country to country. He did not talk so much as narrate. He traced a wavy line, his, and there was usually someone willing to be the random body that he told his stories to.

"I know there's a hospice here. Is this where you talk to the dying?"

"They call it a hospice. They call it a safehold. I don't know what it is. An escort takes me there every day, down in the numbered levels."

He talked about advanced equipment, trained staff. Still, it made him think of twelfth-century Jerusalem, he said, where an order of knights cared for the pilgrims. He imagined at times that he was walking among lepers and plague victims, seeing gaunt faces from old Flemish paintings.

"I think of the bleedings, purgings and baths administered by the knights, the Templars. People from everywhere, the sick and dying, those who tend to them, those who pray for them."

"Then you remember who and where you are."

"I remember who I am. I am the hospitaler. Where I am, this has never mattered."

Ross had also made a reference to pilgrims. This place may not have been intended as the new Jerusalem but people made long journeys to find a form of higher being here, or at least a scientific process that will keep their body tissue from decomposing.

"Does your room have a window?"

"I don't want a window. What's on the other side of a window? Pure dumb distraction."

"But the room itself, if it's like my room, the size of it."

"The room is a solace, a meditation. I can raise my hand and touch the ceiling."

"A monk's cell, yes. And the cloak. I'm looking at the cloak you're wearing."

"It's called a scapular."

"A monk's cloak. But so unmonklike. Aren't such cloaks gray or brown or black or white?"

"Russian monks, Greek monks."

"Okay."

"Carthusian monks, Franciscan monks, Tibetan monks. Monks in Japan, monks in the Sinai desert."

"Your cloak, this one. Where is it from?"

"I saw it draped over a chair. I still visualize the scene."

"You took it."

"The moment I saw it, I knew it was mine. It was predetermined."

I could have asked a question or two. Whose chair, which room, what city, which country? But I understood that this would have been an affront to the man's method of narration.

"What do you do when you're not tending to people in their last hours or days?"

"This is everything I do. I talk to people, I bless them. They ask me to hold their hands, they tell me their lives. Those with strength enough left to talk or to listen."

I watched him get to his feet, a taller man than he'd seemed at first glimpse. The cloak was knee-length and his pajama bottoms flapped as he moved toward the door. He wore high-top sneakers, black-and-white. I did not want to regard him as a comic figure. He was clearly not. I felt, in fact, reduced by his presence, his appearance, by what he said, his trail of happenstance. The cloak was a fetish, a serious one, a monk's scapular, a shaman's cape, carrying what he believed to be spiritual powers.

"Is this tea I'm drinking?"

"Green tea," he said.

I waited for a word or phrase in Uzbek.

Artis said, "It was ten or twelve years ago, surgery, right eye. When it was over they gave me a protective eye shield to wear for a limited time. I sat in a chair at home wearing the shield. There was a nurse, Ross had arranged a nurse, unnecessarily. We followed all the guidelines in the instruction sheet. I slept in the chair for an hour and when I woke up I removed the shield and looked around and everything looked different. I was astonished. What was I seeing? I was seeing what is always there. The bed, the windows, the walls, the floor. But the brightness of it, the radiance. The bedspread and pillow cases, the rich color, the depths of color, something from within. Never before, ever," she said.

Two of us, sitting as we had the day before, and I had to lean in to hear what she was saying. She let time pass before she was ready to continue.

"I'm aware that when we see something, we are getting only a measure of information, a sense, an inkling of what is really there to see. I don't know the details or the terminology but I do know that the optic nerve is not telling the full truth. We're seeing only intimations. The rest is our invention, our way of reconstructing what is actual, if there is any such thing, philosophically, that we can call actual. I know that research is being done here, somewhere in this complex, on future models of human vision. Experiments using robots, lab animals, who knows, people like me."

She was looking directly at me now. She made me see myself, briefly, as the person who was standing here being looked at. Fairly tall man with thick webbed hair, prehistoric hair. This was all I could borrow from the deep probe maintained by the woman in the chair.

She replaced me now with what she'd seen that day.

"But the sight of it, the familiar room now transformed," she said. "And the windows, what did I see? A sky of the sheerest wildest blue. I said nothing to the nurse. What would I say? And the rug, my god, Persian was only a pretty word until now. Am I exaggerating when I say there was something in the shapes and colors, the symmetry of the weave, the warmth, the blush, I don't know what to call it. I became mesmerized by the rug and then by the window frame, white, simply white, but I had never seen white such as this and I was not taking some painkillers that might alter perception, just eyedrops four times a day. A white of enormous depth, white without contrast, I didn't need contrast, white as it is. Am I sure I'm not overstating, inventing outright? I remember clearly what I thought. I thought, Is this the world as it truly looks? Is this the reality we haven't learned how to see? This was not an afterthought. Is this the world that animals see? I thought of this in the first few moments, looking out the window, seeing treetops and sky. Is this the world that only animals are capable of seeing? The world that belongs to hawks, to tigers in the wild."

She gestured throughout but only barely, a hand sifting repeatedly, sorting through the memories, the images.

"I sent the nurse home and went to bed early with the shield on my eye. This was one of the guidelines. In the morning I removed the shield and walked around the house and looked out the windows. My vision was improved but only ordinarily so. The experience was gone, the radiance in things. The nurse returned, Ross called from the airport, I followed the guidelines. It was a sunny day and I took a walk. Or the experience hadn't drifted away and the radiance hadn't faded—it was all simply re-suppressed. What a word. The way we see and think, what our senses will allow, this had to take precedence. What else could I expect? Am I so extraordinary? I returned to see the doctor a few days later. I tried to tell him what I'd seen. Then I looked at his face and stopped."

She continued to speak and seemed at times to lose the pattern, the intonation. She tended to sail away from a word or syllable, eyes searching back for the sensations she was trying to describe. She was all face and hands, body gathered up within the folds of the robe.

"But that's not the end of the story, is it?"

The question pleased her.

"No, it's not."

"Will it happen again?"

"Yes, exactly. This is what I think about. I will become a clinical specimen. Advances will be made through the years. Parts of the body replaced or rebuilt. Note the documentary tone. I've talked to people here. A reassembling, atom by atom. I have every belief that I will reawaken to a new perception of the world."

"The world as it really is."

"At a time that's not necessarily so far off. And this is what I think about when I try to imagine the future. I will be reborn into a deeper and truer reality. Lines of brilliant light, every material thing in its fullness, a holy object."

I'd led her into this song of Life Ever After and now I didn't know how to respond. It was outside my range, all of it. Artis knew the rigors of science. She had worked in a number of countries, taught in several universities. She had observed, identified, investigated and explained many levels of human development. But holy objects, where were they? They were everywhere, of course—in museums and libraries and places of worship and in the excavated earth, in stone and mud ruins, and she'd dug them out and held them in her hands. I imagined her blowing dust from the chipped head of a tiny bronze god. But the future she'd just described was another matter, a purer aura. This was transcendence, the promise of a lyric intensity outside the measure of normal experience.

"Do you know the procedures you'll be undergoing, the details, how they do it."

"I know exactly."

"Do you think about the future? What will it be like to come back? The same body, yes, or an enhanced body, but what about the mind? Is consciousness unaltered? Are you the same person? You die as someone with a certain name and with all the history and memory and mystery gathered in that person and that name. But do you wake up with all of that intact? Is it simply a long night's sleep?"

"Ross and I have a running joke. Who will I be at the reawakening? Will my soul have left my body and migrated to another body somewhere? What's the word I'm looking for? Or will I wake up thinking I'm a fruit bat in the Philippines? Hungry for insects."

"And the real Artis. Where is she?"

"Drifting into the body of a baby boy. The son of local sheepherders."

"The word is *metempsychosis*."

"Thank you."

I didn't know what was around us in the room. All I saw was the woman in the chair.

"Day after tomorrow," I said. "Or is it tomorrow?"

"Doesn't matter."

"I think it's tomorrow. Days have no grip here."

She closed her eyes for a moment and then looked at me as if we were meeting for the first time.

"How old are you?"

"Thirty-four."

"You're just starting."

"Starting what?" I said.

Ross came in from one of the back rooms wearing a gym suit and athletic socks, a man shrouded in lost sleep. He took a chair from the rear wall and positioned it next to the armchair where Artis sat, placing his hand on hers.

"Back then," I said to him, "you used to jog in an outfit like that."

"Back then."

"Maybe not such a designer item."

"Back then I used to smoke a pack and a half a day."

"Was the jogging supposed to counteract the smoking?"

"It was supposed to counteract everything."

Three of us. I realized we hadn't been in the same room for many months. We three. Now, unimaginably, we are here, another kind of convergence, the day before they come and take her. This is how I thought of it. They would come and take her. They would arrive with a gurney that had a reclining back, allowing her to sit up. They would have capsules, vials and syringes. They would fit her with a half-mask respirator.

Ross said, "Artis and I jogged. Didn't we? We used to run along the Hudson River down to Battery Park and back. We ran in Lisbon, remember, six a.m., up that steep street to the chapel and the view. We ran in the Pantanal. In Brazil," he said for my benefit, "on that high path that put us practically in the jungle."

I thought of the bed and the cane. My mother in bed, at the end, and the woman in the doorway, her friend and neighbor, ever nameless, leaning on a cane, a quad cane, a metal cane with four little splayed legs.

Ross talking, recalling things, near to babbling now. Animals and birds they'd seen close-range, and he named them, and plant species, and he named them, and the view from their plane at low altitude swinging over the Mato Grosso.

They would come and take her. They would wheel her into an elevator and take her down to one of the so-called numbered levels. She would die, chemically prompted, in a subzero vault, in a highly precise medical procedure guided by mass delusion, by superstition and arrogance and self-deception.

I felt a surge of anger. I hadn't known until now the depth of my objections to what was happening here, a response obscurely coiled within the rhythms of my father's voice in his desperate reminiscence.

Someone appeared holding a tray, a man with teapot, cups, saucers. He placed the tray on a folding table by my father's chair.

Either way she dies, I thought. At home, in bed, husband and stepson and friends at her side. Or here, in this regimental outpost, where everything happens somewhere else.

The tea brought a pause to the room. We sat quietly until the man was gone. Ross licked his finger and touched the pot. Then he poured, intently, trying hard not to spill.

The tea made me angry all over again. The cups and saucers. The careful pouring.

Artis said, "This place, all of it, seems transitional to me. Filled with people coming and going. Then the others, those who are leaving in one sense, as I am, but staying in another sense, as I am. Staying and waiting. The only thing that's not ephemeral is the art. It's not made for an audience. It's made simply to be here. It's here, it's fixed, it's part of the foundation, set in stone. The painted walls, the simulated doors, the movie screens in the halls. Other installations elsewhere."

"The mannequin," I said.

Ross leaned toward me.

"The mannequin. Where?"

"I don't know where. The woman in the hallway. The woman gesturing, sort of fearfully. The rust-colored woman. Naked woman."

"Where else?" he said.

"I don't know."

"You've seen no other mannequins? No other figures, naked or otherwise?"

"None, absolutely."

"When you arrived," he said. "What did you see?"

"The land, the sky, the buildings. The car driving off."

"What else?"

"I think I told you. Two men at the entrance waiting to escort me. I didn't see them until I approached. Then a security check, thorough."

"What else?"

I thought about what else. I also wondered why we were having this idle talk under these dire circumstances. Is this what happens in the midst of terminal matters? We retreat into neutral space.

"You saw something else, off to the side, maybe fifty meters away, before you entered the building."

"What did I see?"

"Two women," he said. "In long hooded garments."

"Two women in chadors. Of course. Just standing there in the heat and dust."

"The first glimpse of art," he said.

"Never occurred to me."

"Standing absolutely still," he said.

"Mannequins," Artis said.

"To be seen or not seen. Doesn't matter," he said.

"I never imagined they weren't real people. I knew the word. Chadors. Or burqas. Or whatever the other names. This was all I needed to know."

I reached forward and took a teacup from Ross and handed it to Artis. We three. Someone had trimmed and combed her hair, clipping it close to the temples. This seemed almost a rule of order, accentuating the drawn face and stranding the eyes in their dilated state. But I was looking too closely. I was trying to see what she was feeling, in spirit more than body and in the wisping hesitations between words.

She said, "I feel artificially myself. I'm someone who's supposed to be me."

I thought about this.

She said, "My voice is different. I hear it when I speak in a way that's not natural. It's my voice but it doesn't seem to be coming from me."

"Medication," Ross said. "That's all it is."

"It seems to be coming from outside me. Not all the time but sometimes. It's like I'm twins, joined at the hip, and my sister is speaking. But that's not it at all."

"Medication," he said.

"Things come to mind that probably happened. at a certain age we remember things that never too This is different. These things happened but they feel mistakenly induced. Is that what I want to say? An electronic signal gone wrong."

I'm someone who's supposed to be me.

This was a sentence to be analyzed by students of logic or ontology. We waited for her to continue. She spoke in serial fragments now, with stops or rests, and I found myself lowering my head in a sort of prayerful concentration.

"I'm so eager. I can't tell you. To do this thing. Enter another dimension. And then return. For ever more. A word I say to myself. Again and again. So beautiful. For ever more. Say it. And say it. And say it."

The way she cradled her teacup, an heirloom that needed protecting, and to hold it awkwardly or set it down carelessly would betray generational memories.

Ross sitting here in his green-and-white gym suit with possibly matching jockstrap.

"Forevermore," he said.

It was my turn now and I managed to whisper the word. Then her hands began to shake and I put my cup down and reached for her cup and handed it to my father.

I was afraid of other people's houses. After school sometimes a friend might talk me into going to his house or apartment to do our homework together. It was a shock, the way people lived, other people, those who weren't me. I didn't know how to respond, the clinging intimacy of it, kitchen slop, pan handles jutting from the sink. Did I want to be curious, amused, indifferent, superior? Just walking past a bathroom, a woman's stocking draped over the towel rack, pill bottles on the windowsill, some open, some capsized, a child's slipper in the bathtub. It made me want to run and hide, partly from my own fastidiousness. The bedrooms with unmade beds, somebody's socks on the floor, the old woman in night-clothes, barefoot, an entire life gathered up in a chair by the bed, hunched frame and muttering face. Who are these people, minute to minute and year after year? It made me want to go home and stay there.

I thought that I would eventually build a life in opposition to my father's career in global finance. We talked about this, Madeline and I, half seriously. Would I write poetry, live in a basement room, study philosophy, become a professor of transfinite mathematics at an obscure college in west-central somewhere.

Then there was Ross, buying the work of young artists, encouraging them to use the studio he'd built on his property in Maine. Figurative, abstract, conceptual, post-minimal, these were unheralded men and women needing space, time and funding. I tried to convince myself that Ross was using them to smother my response to his bloated portfolio.

In the end I followed the course that suited me. Cross-stream pricing consultant. Implementation analyst—clustered and nonclustered environments. These jobs were swallowed up by the words that described them. The job title was the job. The job looked back at me from the monitors on the desk where I absorbed my situation in full command of the fact that this was where I belonged.

Is it very different at home, or on the street, or waiting at the gate to board a flight? I maintain myself on the pup-pet drug of personal technology. Every touch of a button brings the neural rush of finding something I never knew and never needed to know until it appears at my anxious fingertips, where it remains for a shaky second before disap-pearing forever.

My mother had a roller that picked up lint. I don't know why this fascinated me. I used to watch her guide the device over the back of her cloth coat. I tried to define the word *roller* without sneaking a look in the dictionary. I sat and thought, forgot to keep thinking, then started over, scrib-bling words on a pad, feeling dumber, on and off, into the night and the following day.

A rotating cylindrical device that collects bits of fiber sticking to the surface of a garment.

There was something satisfying and hard-won about this even if I made it a point not to check the dictionary defi-nition. The roller itself seemed an eighteenth-century tool, something to wash horses with. I'd been doing this for a while, attempting to define a word for an object or even a concept. Define *loyalty*, define *truth*. I had to stop before it killed me.

The ecology of unemployment, Ross said on TV, in French, with subtitles. I tried to think about this. But I was afraid of the conclusion I might draw, that the expression was not pretentious jargon, that the expression made sense, opening out into a cogent argument concerning important issues.

When I found an apartment in Manhattan, and found a

job, and then looked for another job, I spent whole weekends walking, sometimes with a girlfriend. There was one so tall and thin she was foldable. She lived on First Avenue and First Street and I didn't know whether her name was spelled Gale or Gail and I decided to wait a while before asking, thinking of her as one spelling one day, the other spelling the next day, and trying to determine whether it made a difference in the way I thought of her, looked at her, talked to her and touched her.

The room in the long empty hall. The chair, the bed, the bare walls, the low ceiling. Sitting in the room and then wandering the halls I could feel myself lapsing into my smallest self, all the vainglorious ideas around me shrunk into personal reverie because what am I in this place but someone in need of self-defense.

The smell of other people's houses. There was the kid who posed for me in his mother's hat and gloves, although it could have been worse. The kid who said that he and his sister had to take turns swabbing lotion on their father's toenails to control some hideous creeping fungus. He thought this was funny. Why didn't I laugh? He kept repeating the word *fungus* while we sat at the kitchen table to do our homework together. A half slice of withered toast slumped in a saucer still damp with spilled coffee. *Sine cosine tangent. Fungus fungus fungus.*

It was the most interesting idea of my life up to now, Gale

or Gail, even if it yielded nothing in the way of insight into the spelling of a woman's name and its effect on the glide of a man's hand over the woman's body.

Systems administrator at a networking site. Human resource planner — global mobility. The drift, job to job, sometimes city to city, was integral to the man I was. I was outside the subject, almost always, whatever the subject was. The idea was to test myself, tentatively. These were mind challenges without a negative subtext. Nothing at stake. Solutions research manager — simulation models.

Madeline, in a rare instance of judgment, leaned across the table in the museum cafeteria where we'd met for lunch.

The vivid boy, she whispered. *The shapeless man.*

The Monk had said that he could get out of the chair and raise a hand and touch the ceiling. In my room I tried to do this and managed, on tiptoes. The moment I sat down I felt a shiver of anonymity.

Then there I am on the subway with Paula from Twin Falls, Idaho, eager tourist and manager of a steakhouse, and there is the man at the other end of the car, addressing the riders, hardship and loss, always a jarring moment, the man who works his way through the train, car to car, jobless, homeless, here to tell his story, paper cup in hand. The eyes of every rider are resolutely blank but we see him, of course, veteran riders, experts in covert looks, as he manages a steady passage through the car despite the train's seismic waves and shakes. Then there is Paula, who watches him openly, who studies him in an analytical way, violating the code. This is rush hour and we are standing, she and I, and I give her a hockey hip check, which she ignores. The subway is the man's total environment, or nearly so, all the way out to Rockaway and up into the Bronx, and he carries with him a claim on our sympathies, even a certain authority that we regard with wary respect, aside from the fact that we would like him to disappear. I put a couple of dollars into his paper cup, hip-checking Paula again, this time for fun, and the man heaves open the door between cars and now I'm the one who's getting a few of the shady glances earlier sent his way.

I walk into the bedroom. There's no wall switch in the room. The lamp sits on the bureau next to the bed. The room is dark. I shut my eyes. Are there other people who shut their eyes in a dark room? Is this a meaningless quirk? Or am I behaving in a way that has a psychological basis, with a name and a history? Here is my mind, there is my brain. I stand a while and think about this.

Ross dragging me along to the Morgan Library to read the spines of fifteenth-century books. He stood gazing at the jeweled cover of the Lindau Gospels in a display case. He arranged access to the second and third tiers, the balconies, after hours, up the hidden staircase, two of us crouching and whispering along the inlaid walnut bookshelves. A Gutenberg Bible, then another, century after century, elegant grillwork crisscrossing the shelves.

That was my father. Who was my mother?

She was Madeline Siebert, originally from a small town in southern Arizona. A cactus on a postage stamp, she called it.

She drapes her coat on a hanger whose hooked upper part she twists so that it fits over the top of the open closet door. Then she runs the roller over the back of the coat. It's satisfying for me to watch this, maybe because I can imagine Madeline taking commonplace pleasure in the simple act of draping her coat on a hanger, strategically arranging the coat on a closet door and then removing the accumulated lint with a roller.

Define *lint*, I tell myself. Define *hanger*. Then I try to do it. These occasions stick and hold, among other bent relics of adolescence.

I returned to the library a few times, regular hours, main floor, tapestry over the mantelpiece, but did not tell my father.

- 6 -

There were three men seated cross-legged on mats with nothing but sky behind them. They wore loose-fitting garments, unmatched, and sat with heads bowed, two of them, the other looking straight ahead. Each man held a container at his side, a squat bottle or can. Two of them had candles in simple holders within reach. After a moment they began, in sequence, left to right, seemingly unplanned, to take up the bottles and pour the liquid on chest, arms and legs. Then two of them, eyes closed, advanced to head and face, pouring slowly. The third man, in the middle, put the bottle to his mouth and drank. I watched his face contort, mouth opening reflexively to allow the fumes to escape. Kerosene or gasoline or lamp oil. He emptied the remaining contents on his head and set the bottle down. They all set the bottles down. The first two men held the lighted candles to their shirtfronts and trouser legs and the third man took a book of matches from his breast pocket and finally, after several failed attempts, managed to strike a flame.

I stepped back from the screen. My face was still twisted in response to the third man's reaction when the kerosene passed through his gullet and entered his system. The burning men, mouths open, swayed above me. I stepped farther back. They were formless, soundless, screaming.

I turned and walked down the hall. The images were everywhere around me, those awful seconds, the distress I felt when the man kept striking the match without getting a flame. I wanted him to light the match. It would be unbearable for him, one blackened match-head after another, to sit between his comrades while they burned.

There was someone standing at the end of the hall, a woman, watching me. Here I was, a lost tourist, unnoticed to this point, a man in retreat from a video screen. The images were still near and pressing but the woman was not looking past me. The screen could have been blank or showing a bare field on a gray day. When I drew near she gestured, faintly, head tilted left, and we turned into a narrow corridor that ended at right angles to another long hall.

She was small, older than I, forties, in a long dress and pink slippers. I said nothing about the burnings. I would respect the format, say nothing, be ready for anything. We walked step for step along the hall. I glanced at the clinging dress in floral design and the woman's dark hair wound tight in a ribboned swirl. She was not a mannequin and this was not a film but I had to wonder whether this interval had any more spread and breadth than just another sequestered moment, bordered by closed doors.

We entered a passageway that dead-ended in what appeared to be a solid surface. My escort recited a series of brief words and this activated a viewing slot in the surface ahead. I took a long step forward and found myself, at an elevated position, staring through the slot at the far wall of a long narrow room.

An oversized human skull was mounted on a pedestal jutting from the wall. The skull was cracked in places, stained with age, a lurid coppery bronze, a drained gray. The eyeholes were rimmed with jewels and the jagged teeth painted silver.

Then there was the room itself, austere, with rock-hewn walls and floor. A man and woman were seated at an oak table with scarred surface. No nameplates, no documents littering the table. They were talking, not necessarily to each other, and facing them were nine people in natural scatter on wooden benches, their backs to me.

I knew the escort would be gone but I corrupted the moment by looking back, like an ordinary person, to check. She was gone, yes, and there was a sliding door about five paces behind me in the process of closing.

The woman at the table was speaking about great human spectacles, the white-clad faithful in Mecca, the hadj, mass devotion, millions, year after year, and Hindus gathered on the banks of the Ganges, millions, tens of millions, a festival of immortality.

She looked frail in a long loose tunic and headscarf, speaking softly and precisely, and I tried to determine the geography of her gracefully accented English, her cinnamon skin.

"Think of the Pope appearing on the balcony above Saint Peter's Square. Enormous numbers of people assembled to be blessed," she said, "to be reassured. The Pope is here to bless their future, to reassure them of the spirit life ahead, beyond the last breath."

I tried to imagine myself among the countless clenched

bodies brought together in awed wonder but could not sustain the notion.

"What we have here is small, painstaking and private. One by one, now and then, people enter the chamber. In an average day, how many? There is no average day. And there is no posturing here. No warping of the body in remorse, submission, obedience, worship. We do not kiss rings or slippers. There are no prayer rugs."

She sat crouched, one hand grasping the other, each considered phrase an emblem of her dedication, so I chose to think.

"But is there a link to older beliefs and practices? Are we a radical technology that simply renews and extends those swarming traditions of everlasting life?"

Someone on the benches turned and looked my way. It was my father, giving me a slow and knowing nod. Here they are, he seemed to be saying, two of the people whose ideas and theories determine the shape of this endeavor. The vital minds, as he'd described them earlier. And the others, they had to be benefactors, as Ross was, the support mechanism, the money people, seated in this stone room, on backless benches, here to learn something about the philosophical heart of the Convergence.

The man began to speak. There was a tone, a ripple somewhere nearby, and his words, in one of the languages of Central Europe, became a smooth digital genderless English.

"This is the future, this remoteness, this sunken dimension. Solid but also elusive in a way. A set of coordinates mapped from space. And one of our objectives is to establish a consciousness that blends with the environment."

He was short and round, high forehead, frizzed hair. He was a blinker, he kept blinking. Talking was an effort and he cranked his hand in rotary motions as he spoke.

"Do we see ourselves living outside time, outside history?" The woman brought us back to earth.

"Hopes and dreams of the future often fail to account for the complexity, the reality of life as it exists on this planet. We understand that. The hungry, the homeless, the besieged, the warring factions and religions and sects and nations. The crushed economies. The wild surges of weather. Can we be impervious to terrorism? Can we ward off threats of cyber-attack? Will we be able to remain truly self-sufficient here?"

The speakers seemed to be directing their remarks somewhere beyond the assembled group. I assumed that there were recording devices, sound and image, outside my range of vision, and that this discussion was intended primarily for the archives.

I also assumed that my presence was meant to be known only to father and son and to the escort with the swirled hair.

They were talking about the end, everybody's end. The woman was looking down now, speaking into the rough wood of the table. I imagined that she was a person who fasted periodically, days without food, sips of water only. I imagined that she'd spent early time in Britain and the U.S., enveloped in her studies, learning how to withdraw, how to conceal herself.

"We are at the mercy of our star," she said.

The sun is an unknown entity. They spoke of solar storms, flares and superflares, coronal mass ejections. The man tried to find adequate metaphors. He cranked his hand in odd synchrony with his references to earth orbit. I watched the woman, bowed down, silent for a time in the setting of billions of years, our vulnerable earth, the comets, asteroids, random strikes, the past extinctions, the current loss of species.

"Catastrophe is our bedtime story."

Blinking man beginning to enjoy himself, I thought.

"To some extent we are here in this location to design a response to whatever eventual calamity may strike the planet. Are we simulating the end in order to study it, possibly to survive it? Are we adjusting the future, moving it into our immediate time frame? At some point in the future, death will become unacceptable even as the life of the planet becomes more fragile."

I saw him at home, head of the table, family dinner, overfurnished room in an old movie. He was a professor, I thought, who'd abandoned the university to pursue the challenge of ideas in this sunken dimension as he'd called it.

"Catastrophe is built into the early brain."

I decided to give him a name. I would give them names, both of them, just for the hell of it, and to stay involved, expand the tenuous role of the concealed man, the surreptitious witness.

"It's an escape from our personal mortality. Catastrophe. It overwhelms what is weak and fearful in our bodies and minds. We face the end but not alone. We lose ourselves in the core of the storm."

I listened carefully to what he was saying. Nicely translated but I didn't believe a word of it. It was a kind of wishful poetry. It didn't apply to real people, real fear. Or was I being small-minded, too limited in perspective?

"We are here to learn the power of solitude. We are here to reconsider everything about life's end. And we will emerge in cyberhuman form into a universe that will speak to us in a very different way."

I thought of several names and rejected them. Then I came up with Szabo. I didn't know if this name was a product of his country of origin but it didn't matter. There were no countries of origin here. I liked the name. It suited his bulging body. Miklos Szabo. It had an earthy savor that contrasted nicely with the programmed voice in translation.

I studied the woman as she spoke. She spoke to no one. She spoke into free space. She needed one name only. No family name, no family, no strong involvements, no hobbies, no particular place she was obliged to return to, no reason not to be here.

The headscarf was her flag of independence.

"Solitude, yes. Think of being alone and frozen in the crypt, the capsule. Will new technologies allow the brain to function at the level of identity? This is what you may have to confront. The conscious mind. Solitude in extremis. Alone. Think of the word itself. Middle English. *All one.* You cast off the person. The person is the mask, the created character in the medley of dramas that constitute your life. The mask drops away and the person becomes *you* in its truest meaning. All one. The self. What is the self? Everything you are, without others, without friends or strangers or lovers or children or streets to walk or food to eat or mirrors in which to see yourself. But are you anyone without others?"

Artis has spoken about being artificially herself. Was this the character, the half fiction who would soon be transformed, or reduced, or intensified, becoming pure self, suspended in ice? I didn't want to think about it. I wanted to think about a name for the woman.

She spoke, with pauses, about the nature of time. What happens to the idea of continuum — past, present, future — in the cryonic chamber? Will you understand days, years and minutes? Will this faculty diminish and die? How human are you without your sense of time? More human than ever? Or do you become fetal, an unborn thing?

She looked at Miklos Szabo, the Old World professor, and I imagined him in a three-piece suit, someone from the 1930s, a renowned philosopher having an illicit romance with a woman named Magda.

"Time is too difficult," he said.

This made me smile. I stood hunched at the viewing slot, which was situated just below eye level, and found myself looking again at the skull across the room, an artifact of the region and possible object of plunder and the last thing I might have expected to find in this environment of scientific approaches to life's end. It was about five times the size of an ordinary human skull and it wore a headpiece, which I hadn't fully registered earlier. This was an imposing skullcap in the shape of many tiny birds, set flat to the skull, a golden flock, wingtips connected.

It looked real, the cranium of a giant, blunt in its deathliness, disconcerting in its craftwork, its silvery grin, a folk art too sardonic to be affecting. I imagined the room empty of people and furniture, rock-walled, stone-cold, and maybe the skull seemed right at home.

Two men entered the room, tall and fair-skinned, twins,

in old workpants and matching gray T-shirts. They stood one to either side of the table and spoke without introduction, each yielding to the other in flawless transition.

"This is the first split second of the first cosmic year. We are becoming citizens of the universe."

"There are questions of course."

"Once we master life extension and approach the possibility of becoming ever renewable, what happens to our energies, our aspirations?"

"The social institutions we've built."

"Are we designing a future culture of lethargy and self-indulgence?"

"Isn't death a blessing? Doesn't it define the value of our lives, minute to minute, year to year?"

"Many other questions."

"Isn't it sufficient to live a little longer through advanced technology? Do we need to go on and on and on?"

"Why subvert innovative science with sloppy human excess?"

"Does literal immortality compress our enduring artforms and cultural wonders into nothingness?"

"What will poets write about?"

"What happens to history? What happens to money? What happens to God?"

"Many other questions."

"Aren't we easing the way toward uncontrollable levels of population, environmental stress?"

"Too many living bodies, too little space."

"Won't we become a planet of the old and stooped, tens of billions with toothless grins?"

"What about those who die? The others. There will always be others. Why should some keep living while others die?"

"Half the world is redoing its kitchens, the other half is starving."

"Do we want to believe that every condition afflicting the mind and body will be curable in the context of our boundless longevity?"

"Many other questions."

"The defining element of life is that it ends."

"Nature wants to kill us off in order to return to its untouched and uncorrupted form."

"What good are we if we live forever?"

"What ultimate truth will we confront?"

"Isn't the sting of our eventual dying what makes us precious to the people in our lives?"

"Many other questions."

"What does it mean to die?"

"Where are the dead?"

"When do you stop being who you are?"

"Many other questions."

"What happens to war?"

"Will this development mark the end of war or a new level of widespread conflict?"

"With individual death no longer inevitable, what will happen to the lurking idea of nuclear destruction?"

"Will all traditional limits begin to disappear?"

"Will the missiles talk themselves out of the launchers?"

"Does technology have a death wish?"

"Many other questions."

"But we reject these questions. They miss the point of

our endeavor. We want to stretch the boundaries of what it means to be human—stretch and then surpass. We want to do whatever we are capable of doing in order to alter human thought and bend the energies of civilization."

They spoke in this manner for a time. They weren't scientists or social theorists. What were they? They were adventurers of a kind that I could not quite identify.

"We have remade this wasteland, this secluded desert shithole, in order to separate ourselves from reasonableness, from this burden of what is called responsible thinking."

"Here, today, in this room, we are speaking into the future, to those who may judge us as brave or quaint or foolish."

"Consider two possibilities."

"We wanted to rewrite the future, all our futures, and ended with a single empty page."

"Or—we were among those few who altered all life on the planet, for all time to come."

I named them the Stenmark twins. They were the Stenmark twins. Jan and Lars, or Nils and Sven.

"The dormants in their capsules, their pods. Those now and those to come."

"Are they actually dead? Can we call them dead?"

"Death is a cultural artifact, not a strict determination of what is humanly inevitable."

"And are they who they were before they entered the chamber?"

"We will colonize their bodies with nanobots."

"Refresh their organs, regenerate their systems."

"Embryonic stem cells."

"Enzymes, proteins, nucleotides."

"They will be subjects for us to study, toys for us to play with."

Sven leaned toward his audience, carrying this last phrase with him, and there was a ripple of amused response from the benefactors.

"Nano-units implanted in the suitable receptors of the brain. Russian novels, the films of Bergman, Kubrick, Kurosawa, Tarkovsky. Classic works of art. Children reciting nursery rhymes in many languages. The propositions of Wittgenstein, an audiotext of logic and philosophy. Family photographs and videos, the pornography of your choice. In the capsule you dream of old lovers and listen to Bach, to Billie Holiday. You study the intertwined structures of music and mathematics. You reread the plays of Ibsen, revisit the rivers and streams of sentences in Hemingway."

I looked again at the woman in the headscarf, unnamed still. She would not be real until I gave her a name. She was sitting upright now, hands resting on the table, eyes closed. She was in a state of meditation. This is what I wanted to believe. Had she listened to a single word spoken by the Stenmarks? Her mind was empty of words, mantras, sacred syllables.

I called her Arjuna, then I called her Arjhana. These were pretty names but they weren't right. Here I was, in a sealed compartment, inventing names, noting accents, improvising histories and nationalities. These were shallow responses to an environment that required abandonment of such distinctions. I needed to discipline myself, be equal to the situation. But when was I ever equal to the situation? What I needed to do was what I was doing.

I listened to the Stenmarks.

"In time a religion of death will emerge in response to our prolonged lives."

"Bring back death."

"Bands of death rebels will set out to kill people at random. Men and women slouching through the countryside, using crude weapons to kill those they encounter."

"Voracious bloodbaths with ceremonial aspects."

"Pray over the bodies, chant over the bodies, do unspeakably intimate things to the bodies."

"Then burn the bodies and smear the ashes on your own bodies."

"Or pray over the bodies, chant over the bodies, eat the edible flesh of the bodies. Burn what remains."

"In one form or another, people return to their death-haunted roots in order to reaffirm the pattern of extinction."

"Death is a tough habit to break."

Nils gestured, fist raised, thumb jutting backwards over his shoulder. He was indicating the skull on the wall. And I understood at once, intuitively, that the big raw bony object was their creation and that these two men, bland in appearance, demonologists in spirit, were the individuals responsible for the look and touch and temperament of the entire complex. This was their design, all of it, the tone and flow, the half-sunken structure itself and everything inside it.

All Stenmark.

This was their aesthetic of seclusion and concealment, all the elements that I found so eerie and disembodying. The empty halls, the color patterns, the office doors that did or did not open into an office. The mazelike moments, time suspended, content blunted, the lack of explanation. I thought of the movie screens that appeared and vanished, the silent films, the mannequin with no face. I thought of my room, the uncanny plainness of it, the nowhereness, conceived and designed as such, and the rooms like it, maybe five hundred or a thousand, and the idea made me feel again that I was dwindling into indistinctness. And the dead, or maybe dead, or whatever they were, the cryogenic dead, upright in their capsules. This was art in itself, nowhere else but here.

The brothers altered their method of address, speaking not to the recording devices but directly to the nine men and women in the audience.

"We spent six years here, without a break, immersed in our work. Then a journey home, brief but fulfilling, and back and forth ever since."

"When the time comes."

"There is a certain inevitability in these words."

"When the time comes, we'll depart finally from our secure northern home to this desert place. Old and frail, limping and shuffling, to approach the final reckoning."

"What will we find here? A promise more assured than the ineffable hereafters of the world's organized religions."

"Do we need a promise? Why not just die? Because we're human and we cling. In this case not to religious tradition but to the science of present and future."

They were speaking quietly and intimately, with a deeper reciprocity than in the earlier exchanges and not a trace of self-display. The audience was stilled, completely fixed.

"Ready to die does not mean willing to disappear. Body and mind may tell us that it is time to leave the world behind. But we will clutch and grasp and scratch nevertheless."

"Two stand-up comics."

"Encased in vitreous matter, refashioned cell by cell, waiting for the time."

"When the time comes, we'll return. Who will we be, what will we find? The world itself, decades away, think of it, or sooner, or later. Not so easy to imagine what will be out there, better or worse or so completely altered we will be too astonished to judge."

They spoke about ecosystems of the future planet, theorizing—a renewed environment, a ravaged environment—and then Lars held up both hands to signal a respite. It took a moment for the audience to absorb the transition but soon the room settled into silence, the Stenmarks' silence. The brothers themselves stared dead ahead, empty-eyed.

The Stenmarks were in their early fifties, this is where I placed them, so thin-skinned and pale that branching blue veins were visible on the backs of their hands, even from where I stood. I decided that they were street anarchists of an earlier era, quietly dedicated to plotting local outrages or larger insurrections, all shaped by their artistic skills, and then I found myself wondering if they were married. Yes, to sisters. I saw them walking in a wooded area, all four, the brothers ahead, then the sisters ahead, a family custom, a game, the distance between the couples coolly measured and carefully maintained. In my half-mad imagining it would be five meters. I made it a point to measure in meters, not in feet or yards.

Lars dropped his arms, the pause ended, the twins resumed speaking.

"Some of you may be back here as well. To witness the

passage of loved ones. And of course you've begun to consider what such a passage might be like for yourselves, one day, each of you, when the time comes."

"We understand that some of the things we've been saying here today may act as disincentives. This is okay. This is the simple truth of our perspective. But do this. Think of money and immortality."

"Here you are, collected, convened. Isn't this what you've been waiting for? A way to claim the myth for yourselves. Life everlasting belongs to those of breathtaking wealth."

"Kings, queens, emperors, pharaohs."

"It's no longer a teasing whisper you hear in your sleep. This is real. You can think beyond the godlike touch of fingertip billions. Take the existential leap. Rewrite the sad grim grieving playscript of death in the usual manner."

This was not a sales pitch. I didn't know what this was, a challenge, a taunt, a thrust at the vanity of the moneyed elect or simply an attempt to tell them what they've always wanted to hear even if they didn't know it.

"Isn't the pod familiar to us from our time in the womb? And when we return, at what age will we find ourselves? Our choice, your choice. Just fill in the blanks on the application form."

I was tired of all this dying and stood away from the viewing slot. But there was no escaping the sound of voices, the brothers reciting a series of Swedish or Norwegian words and then another series of Norwegian or Danish words and then again a series, a list, a litany of German words. I understood a few but not others, not most, nearly none, I realized, as the recitation went on, words in most cases beginning with the syllables *welt*, *wort* or *tod*. This was art that haunts a room, the sonic art of monotone, of incantation, and my response to their voices and all the grave and soaring themes of the afternoon was to drop into a crouch and execute a series of squat-jumps. I jumped and squatted, squatted and jumped, arms thrust upward, five, ten, fifteen times, and then again, down and up, sheer release, and I counted aloud in muttered grunts.

Soon I developed a parallel image of myself as an arboreal ape flinging long hairy arms over its head, hopping and barking in self-defense, building muscles, burning fat.

At some point I became aware that someone else was addressing the audience. It was Miklos, whose surname I'd forgotten—the blinking man in neutered translation speaking now on the subject of being and nonbeing. I kept squatting and jumping.

When I returned to the slot the Stenmark twins were gone, Miklos was still speaking and the woman in the headscarf was positioned as before, seated upright in the chair, hands flat on the table. Her eyes were still closed, everything the same except that now, as I watched, I knew her name. She was Artis. Who else would she be but Artis? That was her name.

I stood in the locked compartment waiting for the sliding door to open. I knew it was wrong to think of it as a sliding door. There had to be an advanced term in use here, a technical word or phrase, but I resisted the implied challenge to consider possibilities.

The escort was waiting when the door slid open. We went along a corridor and then another, wordless once again, both of us, and I expected in minutes to be seeing Ross in his office or suite.

We came to a door and the escort stood and waited. I looked at her and then at the door and we both waited. I realized there was something I wanted, a cigarette. This was a recidivistic need, to grab the semi-crushed pack in my breast pocket, light up quickly, inhale slowly.

I looked at the escort again and understood finally what was happening here. This was my door, the door to my room. I went ahead and opened it and the woman did not leave. I thought of the moment in the stone room when Ross had swiveled on his bench and turned to look at me with a certain expression on his face, a knowingness, father to son, man to man, and in retrospect I realized that he was referring to the situation he'd arranged for me, this situation.

I sat on the bed and watched her undress.

I watched her unravel the ribbon from her hair, slowly, and the hair fall about her shoulders.

I leaned over and took one of her felt slippers in my hand as she eased her foot out of it.

I watched the long dress float down her body to the floor.

I stood and moved into her, smearing her into the wall, imagining an imprint, a body mark that would take days to melt away.

In bed I wanted to hear her speak to me in her language, Uzbek, Kazakh, whatever it was, but I understood that this was an intimacy not suited to the occasion.

I thought of nothing for a time, all hands and body.

Then stillness, and the cigarette to think about again, the one I'd wanted when we were standing outside the door.

I listened to us breathe and found myself imagining the landscape that enclosed us, planing it down, making it abstract, the tender edges of our centeredness.

I watched her dress, slowly, and decided not to give her a name. She blended better, nameless, with the room.

- 7 -

Ross Lockhart is a fake name. My mother mentioned this casually one day when I was nineteen or twenty. Ross told her that he'd taken this action right after he got out of college. He'd been thinking about it for years, first in a spirit of fantasy, then with determination, building a list of names that he inspected critically, with a certain detachment, each deletion bringing him closer to self-realization.

This was the term Madeline used, *self-realization*, speaking in her mild documentary voice as she sat watching TV without the sound.

It was a challenge, he told her. It was an incentive, an inducement. It would motivate him to work harder, think more clearly, begin to see himself differently. In time he would become the man he'd only glimpsed when *Ross Lockhart* was a series of alphabetic strokes on a sheet of paper.

I was standing behind my mother while she spoke. I held a take-out turkey sandwich in one hand, a glass of ginger ale in the other, and the recollection is shaped by the way I stood there thinking and chewing, each bite of the sandwich becoming more deliberate as I concentrated intently on what Madeline was telling me.

I was coming to know the man better now, second by second, word by word, and myself as well. Here was the explanation for the way I walked, talked and tied my shoes. And how interesting it was, in the mere fragments of Madeline's brief narrative, that so many things became so readily apparent. This was the decoding of my baffled adolescence. I was someone I was not supposed to be.

Why hadn't she told me sooner? I waited for her to shrug off the question but she showed no sign of having heard it. All she did was take her eyes off the TV screen long enough to tell me, over her shoulder, what his real name was.

He was born Nicholas Satterswaite. I stared at the far wall and thought about this. I spoke the name inaudibly, moving my lips, over and over. Here was the man laid out before me, balls and all. This was my authentic father, a man who chose to abandon his generational history, all the lives up to mine that were folded into the letters of this name.

When he looks in the mirror he sees a simulated man.

Madeline went back to her TV and I chewed my food and counted the letters. Twenty letters in the full name, twelve in the surname. These numbers told me nothing—what could they tell me? But I needed to get inside the name, work it, wedge myself into it. With the name Satterswaite, who would I have been and what would I have become? I was still, then, at nineteen, in the process of becoming.

I understood the lure of an invented name, people emerging from shadow selves into iridescent fictions. But this was my father's design, not mine. The name Lockhart was all wrong for me. Too tight, too clenched. The solid and decisive Lockhart, the firm closure of Lockhart. The name excluded me. All I could do was peer into it from outside. This is how I understood the matter, standing behind my mother, reminding myself that she did not take the name Lockhart when she married the man.

I wondered what would have happened if I'd learned the truth sooner. Jeffrey Satterswaite. It's possible that I would have been able to stop mumbling, gain weight, add muscle, eat raw clams and get girls to look at me in a spirit of serious appraisal.

But did I really care about origins? It was hard to believe that I would ever make an attempt to explore the genealogy of Satterswaite, to locate the people and places embedded in the name. Did I want to be part of an extended family, somebody's grandson, nephew, cousin?

Madeline and I were each what the other needed. We were singly met. I looked at the TV screen and asked her what there was about the name Nicholas Satterswaite that made him eager to abandon it. The indistinctness of it, she said. The forgettability. The variations in spelling and maybe even pronunciation. From an isolated American viewpoint, the name comes from nowhere and goes nowhere. And then, in contrast, the Anglo-Saxon ancestry of the name. The responsibility this implies. The way his father used the name as a point of reference against which the boy was measured.

But what about the name Lockhart? What is the ancestry? What is the responsibility? She didn't know, I didn't know. Did Ross know?

Onscreen there was a traffic report with live coverage of

cars on an expressway, shot from above. This was the traffic channel, twenty-four hours a day, and after a while, with the sound off and the cars coming into view and passing out of view, never-endingly, the scene floated out of its shallow reality. She watched, I watched, and the scene became apparitional. I stared at the traffic and counted off eight cars and then twelve more, the letters in the real name, first and last, totaling twenty. I kept doing this, eight cars, then twelve. I spelled the name aloud, expecting a possible correction from Madeline. But why would she know or care how the name was spelled?

This is what emerges from that day, maybe that entire year, the way I watched the cars and counted the letters and chewed the sandwich, maple-glazed turkey breast on rye bread from the deli down the street, with never enough mustard.

I'd slept well in body-warmed sheets and wasn't sure whether the meal in front of me was breakfast or lunch. The food itself contained no clue. Why did this make sense? Because the Stenmark Brothers had designed the food units. I imagined their plan. Hundreds of units sized progressively, four tables, sixteen tables, one hundred and fifty-six tables, each unit painstakingly utilitarian, the plates and utensils, the tables and chairs, the food itself, all of it in the spirit of a well-disciplined dream.

I ate slowly, trying to taste the food. I thought of Artis. This is the day when they come and take her. But how do I think about what will happen once her heart stops beating?

How does Ross think about it? I wasn't sure what I wanted to believe, that his trust in the process was genuine or that he'd devised this strength of conviction over time to drown out doubt. Doesn't the fact of imminent death encourage the deepest self-delusion? Artis in the chair sipping tea, the shaky voice and hands, body narrowed to a memory.

The Monk walked in then, nearly startling me, and the small room seemed to gather itself about him. He wore a hooded sweatshirt under the cloak, the hood flopped down behind his neck. Plate, glass and utensils appeared in the slot and he took these to the table. I let him settle into the chair and position the plate.

"I've been hoping to see you again. I have a question."

He paused, not anticipating the question but only wondering if that intrusive noise was a human voice, someone speaking to him.

I waited until he began to eat.

"The screens," I said. "They appear in the halls and disappear into the ceiling. Last screen, last film, a self-immolation. Have you seen it? I thought they were monks. Were they monks? I thought they were kneeling on prayer mats. Three men. Awful to see. Have you seen it?"

"I don't look at the screens. The screens are a distraction. But there are monks, yes, in Tibet, in China, in India, setting themselves aflame."

"In protest," I said.

This remark was too obvious to provoke further comment from the man. I think I expected some credit for raising the subject and for having witnessed the terrible moment itself onscreen, men dying for a cause.

Then he said, "Monks and former monks and nuns and others."

"One of them drank kerosene or gasoline."

"They sit in lotus position or run through the streets. A burning man running through the streets. If I saw such a thing, firsthand, I would run with him. And if he ran screaming, I would scream with him. And when he collapsed, I would collapse."

The sweatshirt was black, sleeves protruding from the cloak. He placed his fork on the plate and sat back. I stopped eating and waited. He could have been sitting in a weary café in a lost corner of some large city, an eccentric figure of the type who is left alone by others, a man often seen but nearly never spoken to. What's his name? Does he have a name? Does he know his name? Why does he dress that way? Where does he live? A man warily regarded by those few who've heard him deliver a monologue on one or another subject. Deep voice, unslurred, interior, and remarks too scattered to warrant a sensible response.

But the Monk wasn't that man, was he? The Monk had a role here. He spoke to men and women who'd been placed in a shelter, a safehold, people in the last days or hours of the only life they'd ever known, and he had no illusions about the sweeping promise of a second life.

He looked at me and I knew what he saw. He saw the figure of a man hunched sort of sideways in a chair. The look told me nothing more than that. The food I was chewing told me it could conceivably be meat.

"I needed to do something, do more than pledge to run alongside, do more than say something or wear a certain garment. How do we stand with others when the things that separate us are imposed at birth, when the separation haunts us and follows us day and night?"

His voice began to carry a storytelling tone, a sense of rec-itation, self-remembrance.

"I decided to make a journey to the sacred mountain in the Tibetan Himalayas. A great white icy pyramid. I learned all the names of the mountain in all the languages. I stud-ied all the histories and mythologies. It took many days of hard travel just to reach the area, well over a week, finally, the last day on foot. Masses of people arriving at the base of the mountain. People crowded into open trucks with bun-dled possessions hanging from the sides and people tum-bling out and milling about and looking up. There's the summit washed in ice and snow. The center of the uni-verse. People with yaks to carry supplies and tents. Tents pitched everywhere. Prayer flags draped everywhere. Men with prayer wheels, men in woolen face masks and old pon-chos. All of us here to make the circumambulation of the high rim at five thousand meters. I was determined to fol-low the trail in the most demanding manner. Take one step and then fall to the ground in body-length prostration. Rise to my feet, take one step, then fall to the ground in body-length prostration. It would take days and then weeks, they told me, for someone not raised and trained in the age-old practice. Thousands of pilgrims every year for two thousand years, walking and crawling beneath the summit. Blizzards in June. Death in the elements. Take one step, then fall to the ground in body-length prostration."

He spoke about levels of devotional stillness, states of

meditation and enlightenment, the fragile nature of their rituals. Buddhists, Hindus, Jains. He wasn't looking at me now. He looked at the wall, spoke to the wall. I sat with fork in hand, suspended between the plate and my mouth. He spoke about abstinence, continence and tantric bliss and I looked at the meatlike specimen at the end of my fork. This was animal flesh that I would chew and swallow.

"I had no guide. I had a yak to carry my tent. Thick brown hairy thing. I kept looking at it. All brown and shaggy, a thousand years old. A yak. I sought advice on whether I should make the trek in clockwise or counterclockwise fashion. There are codes of conduct. The distance would be fifty-two kilometers. Uneven terrain, altitude sickness, snow and fierce wind. Take one step and fall to the ground in body-length prostration. I carried bread, cheese and water. I ascended the main path. I saw no Westerners, there were no Westerners. Men wrapped in horse blankets, men in long robes, men with little wooden shoes fitted to their hands, clogs fitted to their hands to protect against the pebbles and stones as they crawled. Reach the level of circumambulation. Follow the rocky trail. One step or stride and fall to the ground. Body-length prostration. I stood outside my tent and watched them walk and crawl. It was methodical work. They were not showing fervor and holy emotion. They were simply determined, faces and bodies, doing what they'd come here to do, and I watched. There were others standing and resting, others talking, and I watched. I intended to do this, fall to my knees, stretch full-length on the ground, make a mark in the snow with my fingers, speak several meaningless words, inch ahead to the mark made by my fingers, rise to my feet, take a breath, take a step, then fall to my knees again. Parts of my body would lose all feeling in the cold and cutting wind. Those who aspire to total emptiness. Those with foreheads forever cut and bruised from bending to the earth, from kneeling and bowing down and striking the earth. I intended to do this, take a step, fall to my knees, bow to the earth, inch ahead to the mark made by my fingers, speak several nonwords for every step I take."

He kept reminding himself what he'd hoped to do and the repetition was beginning to sound stressed. Could the words reframe the memories? He stopped speaking but kept remembering. I could see him outside his tent, tall man, bareheaded, shrouded in layers of castoff clothing. I knew I wasn't meant to ask whether he'd managed to crawl for an hour or a week. But I responded to the act itself, the principle of it, the man's intentions, so far outside my own fragmented visions, a thing for others, blunt and punishing and filled with steep traditions and simple reverence.

In time he resumed eating and so did I. It occurred to me that my sensitivity to the meat on my fork was completely phony. I didn't feel guilty, even if it was yak meat. I chewed and swallowed. I was beginning to understand that every act I engaged in had to be articulated at some level, had to be performed with the words intact. I could not chew and swallow without thinking of *chew* and *swallow*. Could I blame the Stenmark twins? Maybe I could blame the *room*, my room, the introspective box.

He looked at me again.

"The thinness of contemporary life. I can poke my finger through it."

Then he looked past me and stood with glass in hand and took a last swallow before returning the glass to the table and walking toward the door. I glanced over my shoulder to see a man in the doorway wearing a soccer jersey and sweatpants. The Monk followed him out and I pushed away my table and followed them both.

Pure impulse allows the body to do the thinking. The Monk was aware of my action but said nothing. At the end of the second long hall the escort turned and saw me and he and the Monk exchanged remarks in what I took to be one of the Turkic languages of the region. Then the escort gestured for me to lift my arm waist-high and he took a small pointed instrument from a narrow pocket in his trousers and touched it to the disk on my wristband. I took this to mean that I could now gain admission to areas previously restricted.

We three entered an enclosure and as the access door slid shut behind us I became faintly aware of motion that may have been horizontal, a whispered glide at a speed that I could not estimate. Time seemed also beyond my ability to measure. There was a sense of temporal blur and it could have been seconds or possibly minutes before we were inserted into a vertical shaft, proceeding downward, so I imagined, into the numbered levels. The effect was a free-floating sensation, nearly out-of-body, and if the two others spoke I didn't hear them.

A paneled door opened and we walked down a passageway into a large low shadowed space. It was almost librarylike, with rows of partitioned cubicles or stalls similar to carrels for private study. The Monk paused here, then reached back over his shoulder for the black hood, the sweatshirt hood, fitting it snugly over his head. I decided to interpret this as a ceremonial moment.

I followed him down several steps into the array of carrels and saw that they held patients rather than students, people seated or strapped upright, others lying face up and utterly still, eyes opened, eyes closed, and empty carrels as well, a fair number. This was the Monk's workplace, the hospice, and I went where he went, along a network of aisles, with carrels on either side. I could make out the texture of the nearest wall, coarse-grained, in neutral colors, bands of black and gray swabbed on, intermixed, and the scant lighting and low ceiling and huddled men and women, the general dimensions of the area, and I could not find a category, something Stenmarklike to attach to the setting.

I looked at the patients in their chairs or beds, which were neither chairs nor beds. They were a kind of padded stool or soft bench and it wasn't easy to tell which individuals were asleep, which were tranquilized, which under the influence of anesthesia at one or another level. At times, here and there, an individual looked completely and full-bloodedly aware.

The Monk stopped at the end of the aisle we were in and turned toward me just as I turned the other way to check on the presence of our escort, who was not there.

"We're waiting," he said.

"Yes, I understand."

What did I understand? That I was feeling hemmed in, close to being trapped, and I asked the Monk about his prevailing frame of mind, the disposition he experienced when he was here.

"I don't have a disposition."

I asked him about the stalls, the carrels.

"I call them cribs."

I asked him what we were waiting for.

"Here they come," he said.

There were five individuals in dark smocks, two with shaved heads, moving along the aisles in our general direction. They were attendants or orderlies or paramedics or escorts. They stopped at a nearby carrel, two of them checking devices on the headboard, one of them speaking to the patient. Three of the individuals then led the departure, single-file, and the two bald orderlies pushed the wheeled carrel along behind them. I thought of the other patients and tried to imagine the tense anticipation they felt, their turns coming, as they watched this odd troop proceed along the aisle and into shadow.

When I turned toward the Monk he was already engaged with the person in a nearby carrel. It was a woman, seated, and he spoke to her quietly in what I took to be a rambling sort of Anglo-Russian, leaning close, his hands folded over hers. The words were an effort for him to summon but the woman's head bobbed in response and I knew it was time for me to leave the man to his task.

The Monk in his old rutted cloak, his scapular.

I wandered for a while, expecting to be stopped. I thought I might talk to someone among the bodies-in-waiting. No sign of attendants giving massages or monitoring heart rates and no sound of therapeutic music. I began to think I'd blundered my way into a half-empty warehouse of bodies, barely an eye blinking or a finger twitching.

I realized I was shivering. It was only a slight tremble but it made me look around and then up and down, dumbly, seeing the same neutral tones in all directions, states of gray, modest and somber, in-between, the ceiling lower here, the lighting dimmer, and maybe it was a bomb shelter that the Stenmarks had in mind.

I walked along the aisles glancing at the few patients in this sector. I thought the word itself was all wrong. But what were they if they weren't patients? Then I thought of the words that Ross had used in his description of the prevailing tone here. *Reverence* and *awe*. Is this what I was seeing? I saw eyes, hands, hair, skin tone, facial configuration. Races and nations. And not patients but subjects, submissive and unstirring. I stood before a sedated woman wearing eye shadow. I did not see peace, comfort and dignity, only a person under the authority of others.

I stopped alongside a robust man seated in his carrel. He wore a knit shirt and resembled a fellow on a golf course plunked down in his cart. I stood in front of him and asked how he was feeling.

He said, "Who are you?"

I told him I was a visitor eager to be educated. I said he looked pretty healthy. I said I was curious about the time he'd spent here and how much longer it would be before he was taken wherever they would take him.

He said, "Who are you?"

I said, "Don't you feel the chill, the damp air, the tight space?"

He said, "I'm looking right through you."

Then I saw the boy. I knew at once that it was the same kid I'd seen in a motorized wheelchair in one of the hallways, accompanied by two hollow-bodied escorts. Here, he was seated in a carrel, shiny and very still, positioned almost sculpturelike, contrapposto, head and shoulders twisted one way, hips and legs the other.

I didn't know what to say. I said my name. I spoke to him softly, careful not to crowd him. I asked him how old he was and where he was from.

Head turned left, eyes swiveling up and to the right, where I was standing. He seemed to be thinking his way into my presence here, possibly even remembering our momentary encounter. Then he began to speak, or to produce what sounded like random noise, a series of indistinct sounds that were not mumbled or stuttered but only, somehow, broken. He was expressing his thoughts but I wasn't able to detect a trace of any known language, or a nuance of meaning, and he showed no awareness that he could not be understood.

He was motionless except for his mouth and eyes and I moved to a point where he did not have to stretch his range of vision. I did not speak again but only stood and listened. And I did not try to guess his country of origin, or who had brought him here, or when he would be taken to the chamber.

The only thing I did was take his hand and wonder how much time remained to him. In his physical impairment, the nonalignment of upper and lower body, in this awful twistedness I found myself thinking of the new technologies that would one day be applied to his body and brain, allowing him to return to the world as a runner, a jumper, a public speaker.

How could I fail to consider the idea, even in my deep skepticism?

I don't know how long I remained. When he stopped speaking, abruptly, and dropped into immediate sleep, I lifted my hand from his and went looking for the Monk.

I made my way through the sector and was relieved to see the Monk standing and gesturing above someone's carrel and it occurred to me that I might give him a name, as I'd done with the speakers in the stone room. But a name, in his case a fictitious birth name, would be dead weight. He was the Monk and he was addressing the subjects, one by one, in their carrels, their cribs.

I thought of the boy. I realized it was the boy that I should have named. It would not have helped me interpret his speech, the sounds that bounced out of him, but I would have perceived something as I listened, a fragment of identity, a tiny shaping element to ease the questions that whirled about him.

I stood near the Monk and tried to listen to what he said to those he approached. At one point, in Spanish, he told an elderly woman that she was blessed to be lying here, in peace, and to be thinking about her mother, who had been spread-bodied, in pain, to give birth to her. I was able to understand this but not everything he said to everyone until he told a middle-aged man, in English, that the place where he would reside, in a preserved state, was very deep in the earth — deeper still than this cloistered hall. Possibly even safe from world's end. The Monk spoke enthusiastically about world's end.

The Monk in his sweatshirt hood, his cowl.

We walked together toward the passageway where we'd entered and I asked him several questions about the procedures here.

"This is the safehold, the waiting place. They're waiting to die. Everyone here dies here," he said. "There is no arrangement to import the dead in shipping containers, one by one, from various parts of the world, and then place them in the chamber. The dead do not sign up beforehand and then die and then get sent here with all the means of preservation intact. They die here. They come here to die. This is their operational role."

This is all he had to say. When we entered the enclosure from which we'd be delivered to our level, there was no sign of our escort and the Monk showed no interest in waiting for him to appear. In our soft ascent I began to understand what this meant, that there was no one, at least for now, who might return the disk on my wristband to its restrictive function.

I said nothing, the Monk said nothing.

When I walked into my room I looked at whatever there was to see and touch and then I spoke the word for each thing. There was a bottle of hand sanitizer in the pygmy bathroom that hadn't been there before and this messed up my immersion in the plain words for the familiar objects. I looked in the mirror over the sink and said my name aloud. Then I went looking for my father.

- 8 -

Ross wasn't in the office he'd been using. Nothing was in the office. Desk and chairs gone, computer equipment, wall charts, standing tray with glasses gone, whiskey bottle gone. This was briefly unsettling but then not so strange. The time was near for Artis to be taken down and for Ross to be returning to the world he'd made.

I went to the suite expecting to see Artis in her chair, in robe and slippers, hands folded in lap. What would I say to her and how would she look, thinner, paler, and would she be unable to speak to me or to see me sitting there facing her?

But it was my father in the chair. I had to pause to assemble the information, Ross barefoot in a T-shirt and designer jeans. He didn't look at me when I entered but simply noted a figure wandering into his line of vision, another presence in the room. I sat on the bench nearby, facing him as I'd faced her, only, now, feeling regret over the fact that I'd missed seeing her one last time.

"I thought you'd let me know."

"It hasn't happened."

"Again. Hasn't happened again. Where is she?"

"In the bedroom."

"And it will happen tomorrow. Is that what you're going to tell me."

I got up and walked over to the bedroom door and opened it and there she was, in bed, under the covers, eyes opened. Her hands rested above the blanket and I approached slowly and took one hand and held it and then waited.

She said, "Jeffrey."

"Yes, it's him, it's me."

"Make up your mind," she whispered.

I smiled and said that in her presence I tended to be him rather than me. But this is all there was. Her eyes closed and I waited for a time before releasing her hand and leaving the room.

Ross was walking wall to wall, hands in pockets, not appearing to be deep in thought so much as following the conditioning routine of an innovative fitness system.

"Yes, it will happen tomorrow," he said casually.

"This is not some game that the doctors are playing with Artis."

"Or that I'm playing with you."

"Tomorrow."

"You'll be alerted early. Be here, this room, first thing, first light."

He kept pacing and I sat watching.

"Is she really at the point where this has to be done now? I know she's ready for it, eager to test the future. But she thinks, she speaks."

"Tremors, spasms, migraines, lesions on the brain, nervous system in collapse."

"Sense of humor intact."

"There's nothing left for her on this level. She believes that and so do I."

I kept watching him. A new fitness system that stressed the viability of bare feet and hands-in-pockets. I asked him, simply, how many times he'd been here, to the complex, to look and to listen.

"Five times counting this visit. Twice before with Artis. The experience tightened my idea of myself. I let certain preoccupations fall away. I shrugged them off. I began to think more inwardly."

"And Artis."

"And Artis, the one who made me understand how the scope and intensity of such an enterprise can become part of someone's daily life, minute to minute. Wherever I was, wherever I went, or just eating a meal, or trying to get to sleep, this was in my mind, in my skin. People like to say of unique occurrences, implausible situations—people say that no one could make this up. But someone made this up, all of it, and here we are."

"Maybe I'm too limited in vision. Inadequate to the experience. All I seem to be doing is relating what I've seen and heard in these few days to what I already know. There's a chain of reverse associations. The cryonic pod, the tube, the capsule, the toll booth, the phone booth, the ticket booth, the shower stall, the sentry box."

He said, "You're forgetting the outhouse."

He took his hands out of his pockets and walked faster for a number of minutes and then stopped and stood against the far wall taking exaggerated breaths, loud and deep. He came back to the chair and spoke quietly now.

"I'll tell you what's unsettling."

"I'm listening."

"Men are supposed to die first. Shouldn't the man die first? Don't you have this kind of sixth sense? We feel it within us. We die, they live on. Isn't this the natural order?"

"There's another way to look at it," I said. "The women die, leaving the men free to kill each other."

He seemed to enjoy the remark.

"Obliging women. Deferring to the needs of their men. Ever-accommodating, self-sacrificing, loving and supporting. Madeline. That was her name, wasn't it? Your mother?"

I waited, uneasily.

"Do you know that she stabbed me once? No, you don't know this. She never told you. Why would she? She stabbed me in the shoulder with a steak knife. I was at the table eating the steak and she came up behind me and stabbed me in the shoulder. Not a four-star-restaurant steak knife with macho overtones but it hurt like hell anyway. It also made me bleed all over a new shirt. That's all. Nothing more. I didn't go to the emergency room, I went to the bathroom, ours, and doctored it pretty well. I didn't call the cops either. Just a family disagreement although I don't recall now what the disagreement was. Getting rid of a nice new shirt, that's what I recall. Maybe she stabbed me because she hated the shirt. Maybe she was getting even with the shirt by stabbing me. These are things in a marriage. Nobody knows what's in the marriage next door. It's tough enough figuring out what's in your own marriage. Where were you at the time? I don't know, you were beddy-bye, or at summer camp, or walking the dog. Didn't we have a dog for two weeks? Anyway I made it a point to throw away the steak knife because I didn't think it would be a suitable utensil for us to use again even if we'd all gathered together and devised scrubbing methods that would render the thing blood-free and germ-free and memory-free. Even if we'd all agreed on the most fastidious methods. You and I and Madeline."

There was something I hadn't realized until now. Ross had shaved his beard.

"That night we slept in the same bed, as usual, she and I, and said little or nothing, also as usual."

His tone of voice in this final remark was softer, somewhat haunted. I wanted to believe that he'd reached another tier of reminiscence, deeper and not so bleak and suggesting an element of regret and loss, and maybe a share of the blame.

He went back to the wall and began to pace, arms swinging faster and higher, breath coming in regulated bursts. I didn't know what to do, or say, or where to go. These were his four walls, not mine, and I began to think of the mindless hours, time zones home, the steady murmur of return.

When I was fourteen I developed a limp. I didn't care if it looked fake. I practiced at home, walking haltingly room to room, tried not to revert to normal stride after I rose from a chair or got out of bed. It was a limp set between quotation marks and I wasn't sure whether it was intended to make me visible to others or just to myself.

I used to look at an old photograph of my mother, Madeline in a pleated dress, age fifteen, and I'd feel sad. But she wasn't ill, she hadn't died.

When she was at work I'd take a phone message for her and write down the information, making certain to tell her when she came home. Then I waited for her to return the call. Actively watched and waited. I reminded her once and then again that the lady from the dry cleaner had called and she looked at me with a certain expression, the one that said I am looking at you this way because there is no point wasting words when you can recognize the look and know that it says what should not need to be said. It made me nervous, not the look but the phone call waiting to be returned. Why isn't she calling back. What is she doing that's so important that she can't call back. Time is passing, the sun is setting, the person is waiting, I am waiting.

I wanted to be bookish and failed. I wanted to steep myself in European literature. There I was in our modest garden apartment, in a nondescript part of Queens, steeping myself in European literature. The word *steep* was the whole point. Once I decided to steep myself, there was no need to read the work. I tried at times, made an effort but failed. I was technically unsteeped but also ever-intentioned, seeing myself in the chair reading a book even as I sat in the chair watching a movie on TV with French or German subtitles.

Later, living elsewhere, I visited Madeline fairly often and began to notice that when we ate a meal together she used paper napkins instead of cloth because, understandably, it was only her, just another solitary meal, or only her and me, which came to the same thing, except that after she set out a plate, fork and knife next to the paper napkin she avoided using the napkin, paper or not, keeping it unsmudged, using a facial tissue sticking out of a nearby box, Kleenex Ultra Soft, *ultra doux*, to wipe her mouth or fingers, or walking over to the roll of paper towels in the rack above the kitchen sink and tearing off a segment of a single towel and wiping her mouth on it and then folding the segment over the smudged part and bringing it to the table to use again, leaving the paper napkin untouched.

The limp was my faith, my version of flexing muscles or jumping hurdles. After the early days of its separateness, the limp began to feel natural. At school the kids mainly smirked or mimicked. A girl threw a snowball at me but I interpreted this as a playful gesture and responded accordingly, clutching my groin and wagging my tongue. The limp was something to cling to, a circular way to recognize myself, step by step, as the person who was doing this. Define *person*, I tell myself. Define *human*, define *animal*.

Madeline went to the theater occasionally with a man named Rick Linville, who was short, friendly and beefy. It was clear to me that there was no romance. Aisle seats, that's what there was. My mother did not like to be hemmed in and required a seat on the aisle. She did not dress for the theater. She stayed plain, always, face, hands, hair, while I tried to find a name for her friend that was suited to his height, weight and personality. Rick Linville was a skinny name. She listened to my alternatives. First names first. Lester, Chester, Karl-Heinz. Toby, Moby. I was reading from a list I'd made at school. Morton, Norton, Rory, Roland. She looked at me and listened.

Names. Fake names. When I learned the truth about my father's name, I was on holiday break from a large midwestern college where all the shirts, sweaters, jeans, shorts and skirts of all the students parading from one place to another tended to blend on sunny football Saturdays into a single swath of florid purple-and-gold as we filled the stadium and bounced in our seats and waited to be tracked by the TV cameras so we could rise and wave and yell and after twenty minutes of this I began to regard the plastic smile on my face as a form of self-inflicted wound.

I didn't think of the untouched paper napkin as a marginal matter. This was the unseeable texture of a life except that I was seeing it. This is who she was. And as I came to know who she was, seeing it with each visit, my sense of attentiveness deepened. I tended to overinterpret what I saw, yes, but I saw it often and could not help thinking that these small moments were far more telling than they might appear to be, although I wasn't sure what they told, the paper napkin, the utensils in the cabinet drawer, the way she removes the clean spoon from the drain basket and makes it a point not to place it in the cabinet drawer on top of all the other clean spoons of the same size but beneath the others in order to maintain a chronology, a proper sequence. Most-recently-used spoons, forks and knives at the bottom, next-to-be-used at the top. Utensils in the middle would work their way to the top as those at the top were used and then cleaned and dried and placed at the bottom.

I wanted to read Gombrowicz in Polish. I didn't know a word of Polish. I only knew the writer's name and kept repeating it silently and otherwise. Witold Gombrowicz. I wanted to read him in the original. The phrase appealed to me. Read him in the original. Madeline and I at dinner, there we are, some kind of muggy stew in cereal bowls, I'm fourteen or fifteen and keep repeating the name softly, Gombrowicz, Witold Gombrowicz, seeing it spelled out in my head and saying it, first name and last—how could you not love it—until my mother elevates her gaze from the bowl and delivers a steely whisper, *Enough.*

She was adept at knowing what time it was. No wristwatch, no clock in view. I might test her, without warning, when we were taking a walk, she and I, block by block, and she was always able to report the time within a three- or four-minute margin of variation. This was Madeline. She watched the traffic channel with accompanying weather reports. She stared at the newspaper but not necessarily at the news. She watched a bird land on the rail of the small balcony that jutted from the living room and she kept watching, motionless, the bird also watching whatever it was watching, still, sunlit, alert, prepared to flee. She hated the small orange day-glo price stickers on grocery cartons, medicine bottles and tubes of body lotion, a sticker on a peach, unforgivably, and I'd watch her dig her thumbnail under the sticker to remove it, get it out of her sight, but more than that, to adhere to a principle, and sometimes it took minutes before she was able to pry the thing loose, calmly, in fragments, and then roll it in her fingers and toss it in the trash can under the kitchen sink. She and the bird and the way I stood and watched, a sparrow, sometimes a goldfinch, knowing if I moved my hand the bird would fly off the rail and the fact of knowing this, the possibility of my intercession, made me wonder if my mother would even notice that the bird was gone, but all I did was stiffen my posture, invisibly, and wait for something to happen.

I'd take a phone message from her friend Rick Linville and tell her he'd called and then wait for her to call back. Your theater friend Rick, I'd say, and then recite his phone number, once, twice, three times, out of spite, watching her put the groceries away, methodically, like the forensic preservation of someone's war-torn remains.

She cooked sparse meals for us and drank wine rarely — and never, to my knowledge, hard liquor. Sometimes she let me prepare a meal while she issued casual instructions from the kitchen table, where she sat doing work she'd brought home from the office. These were the simple timelines that shaped the day and deepened her presence. I wanted to believe that she was my mother far more compellingly than my father was my father. But he was gone so there was no point matching them up.

She wanted the paper napkin untouched. She was substituting paper for cloth and then judging the paper to be indistinguishable from cloth. I told myself there would eventually be a lineage, a scheme of direct descent — cloth napkins, paper napkins, paper towels, facial tissues, sneeze tissues, toilet tissues, then down into the garbage for scraps of reusable plastic packaging minus the day-glo price stickers, which she'd already removed and crumpled.

There was another man whose name she would not tell

me. She saw him on Fridays only, twice a month maybe, or only once, and never in my presence, and I imagined a married man, a wanted man, a man with a past, a foreigner in a belted raincoat with straps on the shoulders. This was a cover-up for the uneasiness I felt. I stopped asking questions about the man and then the Fridays ended and I felt better and started asking questions again. I asked whether he wore a belted raincoat with straps on the shoulders. It's called a trench coat, she said, and there was something final in her voice so I decided to terminate the man in the crash of a small plane off the coast of Sri Lanka, formerly Ceylon, body unrecovered.

Certain words seemed to be located in the air ahead of me, within arm's reach. *Bessarabian, penetralia, pellucid, falafel.* I saw myself in these words. I saw myself in the limp, in the way I refined and nurtured it. But I killed the limp whenever my father showed up to take me to the Museum of Natural History. This was the estranged husbands' native terrain and there we were, fathers and sons, wandering among the dinosaurs and the bones of human predecessors.

She gave me a wristwatch and on my way home from school I kept checking the minute hand, regarding it as a geographical marker, a sort of circumnavigation device indicating certain places I might be approaching somewhere in the northern or southern hemisphere depending on where the minute hand was when I started walking, possibly Cape Town to Tierra del Fuego to Easter Island and then maybe to Tonga. I wasn't sure whether Tonga was on the semicircular route but the name of the place qualified it for inclusion, along with the name Captain Cook, who sighted Tonga or visited Tonga or sailed back to Britain with a Tongan on board.

When the marriage died, my mother began working full-time. Same office, same boss, a lawyer who specialized in real estate. She'd studied Portuguese in her two years of college and this was useful because a number of the firm's clients were Brazilians interested in buying apartments in Manhattan, often for investment purposes. Eventually she began to handle the details of transactions among the seller's attorney, the mortgage firm and the managing agent. People buying, selling, investing. Father, mother, money.

I understood years later that the strands of attachment could be put into words. My mother was the loving source, the reliable presence, a firm balance between me and my little felonies of self-perception. She did not press me to be more social or to spend more time on homework. She did not forbid me to watch the sex channel. She said that it was time for me to resume a normal stride. She said that the limp is a heartless perversion of true infirmity. She told me that the pale crescent at the base of the fingernail is called the lunula, the *loon*-ya-la. She told me that the indentation in skin between the nose and the upper lip is called the philtrum. In the ancient Chinese art of face-reading, the philtrum represents such-and-such. She could not remember exactly what.

I decided that the man she saw on Fridays was probably Brazilian. He was more interesting to me than Rick Linville, who had a name and a shape, but there was always the implicit subject of how the Friday evenings ended, what they said and did together, in English and Portuguese, which

I needed to keep nameless and shapeless, and then there was her silence concerning the man himself, and maybe it wasn't even a man. That's the other thing I found myself confronting. Maybe it wasn't even a man. Things that come to mind, out of nowhere or everywhere, who knows, who cares, so what. I took a walk around the corner and watched the senior citizens play tennis on the asphalt court.

Then came the day and year when I glanced at a magazine on a newsstand in an airport somewhere and there was Ross Lockhart on the cover of *Newsweek* with two other godheads of world finance. He wore a pinstriped suit and restyled hair and I called Madeline so I could refer to his serial killer's sideburns. Her neighbor picked up the phone, the woman with the metal cane, the quad cane, and she told me that my mother had suffered a stroke and that I must come home at once.

In memory the actors are locked in position, unlifelike. Me in a chair with a book or magazine, my mother watching TV without the sound.

Ordinary moments make the life. This is what she knew to be trustworthy and this is what I learned, eventually, from those years we spent together. No leaps or falls. I inhale the little drizzly details of the past and know who I am. What I failed to know before is clearer now, filtered up through time, an experience belonging to no one else, not remotely, no one, anyone, ever. I watch her use the roller to remove lint from her cloth coat. Define *coat*, I tell myself. Define *time*, define *space*.

• • •

"You shaved your beard. Took me a few minutes to notice. I was just getting adjusted to the beard."

"There are things I've been thinking about."

"Okay."

"Things I've been struggling with for some time," he said. "Then it became clear. I understood that there's something I have to do. It's the only answer."

"Okay."

Ross in the armchair, Jeff on the cushioned bench, two tense men in conversation, and Artis in the bedroom waiting to die.

He said, "I'm going with her."

Did I know what he meant, instantly, reading it in his face, and then did I pretend to be confused?

"You're going with her."

It was necessary for me to repeat those words. *Going with her.* At some level I understood that my role was to think and speak along conventional lines.

"You mean being with her when they take her down and do what they have to do. You want to monitor the proceedings."

"Going with her, joining her, sharing it, side by side."

There was a long wait for one of us to resume speaking. The simple fact of these words, the immense force gathering behind them, turning me inside out.

"I know what you're saying. But the questions I'm supposed to ask don't seem to be coming."

"I've been thinking about this for some time."

"You already said that."

"I don't want to lead the life I'll be leading without her."

"Isn't this what everyone feels when someone close, someone intimately attached, is about to die?"

"I can only be the man I am."

That was nice, with a tinge of helplessness.

Another long silence, Ross looking into space. He is going with her. It denied everything he'd ever said and done. It made a comic strip of his life, or of mine. Was this a bid for redemption, some kind of spiritual deliverance after all the acquisitions, all the wealth he'd managed for others and accumulated for himself, the master market strategist, owner of art collections and island retreats and super-midsize jets. Or was he suffering a brief spell of madness with long-range consequences?

What else?

Could it simply be love? All those unconditional words. Had he earned them, man with a fake name, half husband, missing father. I told myself to stop the rant, the spinning inner grievance. A man of his resources choosing to be a frozen specimen in a capsule in a storage facility twenty years before his natural time.

"Aren't you the man who lectured me on the shortness of the human life span? Our lives measured in seconds. And now you cut it even shorter, by choice."

"I'm ending one version of my life to enter another and far more permanent version."

"In the current version, you have regular health checks, I assume. Of course you do. And what do the doctors say? Is there one doctor, a little gimpy man with bad breath? Did he tell you there's something potentially serious going on in your body?"

He waved away the idea.

"He sent you for tests, then more tests. Lungs, brain, pancreas."

He looked at me and said, "One dies, the other has to die. It happens, doesn't it?"

"You're a healthy man."

"Yes."

"And you're going with her."

"Yes."

I wasn't finished looking for low motives.

"Tell me this. Have you committed crimes?"

"Crimes."

"Enormous frauds. Doesn't this happen all the time in your line of work? Investors get swindled. What else? Enormous sums of money get transferred illegally. What else? I don't know. But these are reasons, right, for a man to disappear."

"Stop babbling like a fucking idiot."

"Stop babbling, okay. But one more idiotic question. Aren't you supposed to die *before* they do the freezing?"

"There's a special unit. Zero K. It's predicated on the subject's willingness to make a certain kind of transition to the next level."

"In other words they help you die. But in this case, your case, the individual is nowhere near the end."

"One dies, the other has to die."

Again, silence.

"I'm having a completely unreal experience. I'm looking at you and trying to understand that you're my father. Is that right? The man I'm looking at is my father."

"This is unreal to you."

"The man who is telling me these things is my father. Is that right? And he says he is going with her. 'I am going with her.' Is that right?"

"Your father, yes. And you're my son."

"No, no. I'm not ready for that. You're getting ahead of me. I'm doing my best to recognize the fact that you're my father. I'm not ready to be your son."

"Maybe you ought to think about it."

"Give me time. In time I may be able to think about it."

I had a sense of being outside myself, aware of what I was saying but not saying it so much as simply hearing it.

"Do yourself a favor," he said. "Listen to what I have to say."

"I think you've been brainwashed. You're a victim of these surroundings. You're a member of a cult. Don't you see it? Simple old-fashioned fanaticism. One question. Where is the charismatic leader?"

"I've made provisions for you."

"Do you understand how this reduces me?"

"The future will be secure. Your choice to accept or reject. You'll leave here tomorrow knowing this. A car will pick you up at noon. The flight arrangements are made."

"I'm shamed by this, totally diminished."

"You'll be met along the way by a colleague of mine who will provide all the details, all the documents you may need, a secure file, to help you decide what it is you want to do from this day on."

"My choice."

"Accept, reject."

I tried to laugh.

"Is there a time limit?"

"All the time you need. Weeks, months, years."

He was still looking at me. This is the man who was walking barefoot, wall to wall, arms swinging, ten minutes ago. It made sense now. The prisoner pacing his cell, thinking last thoughts, having second thoughts, wondering if there's a toilet in the special unit.

"And Artis has known this for how long?"

"When I knew it, she knew it. Once I was certain, I told her."

"And she said what?"

"Try to understand that she and I share a life. The decision I made only deepens the bond. She said nothing. She simply looked at me in a way I can't begin to describe. We want to be together."

I had nothing to say to this. Other subjects eluded me as well except for one detail.

"Those in authority here. They will carry out your wishes."

"We don't need to get into that."

"They will do this for you. Because it's you. Simple injection, serious criminal act."

"Let it go," he said.

"And in return, what? You've framed wills and trusts and testaments granting them certain resources and holdings well beyond what you've already given them."

"Finished?"

"Is it outright murder? Is it a form of assisted suicide that's horribly premature? Or is it a metaphysical crime that needs to be analyzed by philosophers?"

He said, "Enough."

"Die a while, then live forever."

I didn't know what else to say, what to do, where to go. Three, four, five days, however long I'd been here—time compressed, time drawn tight, overlapping time, dayless, nightless, many doors, no windows. I understood of course that this place was located at the far margins of plausibility. He'd said so himself. No one could make this up, he'd said. This was the point, their point, in three dimensions. A literal landmark of implausibility.

"I need a window to look out of. I need to know there's something out there, out beyond these doors and walls."

"There's a window in the spare room next to the bedroom."

I said, "Never mind," and remained on the bench.

I'd mentioned a window because I assumed there would not be a window. Maybe I wanted one more thing to work against me. Pity the trapped man.

"You thought you knew who your father was. Isn't this what you meant when you said you felt reduced by this decision?"

"I don't know what I meant."

He told me that I hadn't done anything yet. Hadn't lived yet. All you do is pass the time, he said. He mentioned my determined drift, week to week, year to year. He wanted to know if this was threatened by what he'd just told me. Job to job, city to city.

"You're taking too much credit," I said.

He was peering into my face.

The counter career, he said. The noncareer. Will this have to change now? He called it my little church of noncommitment.

He was getting angrier. Didn't matter what he said. Words themselves, the momentum of his voice, this was shaping the moment.

"The women you've known. Do you get interested in them according to guidelines you've entered on your smartphone? Can't last, won't last, never last."

She stabbed him. My mother stabbed this man with a steak knife.

My turn now.

"Going with her. You're turning Artis into a mirage," I said. "You're walking straight into a distortion of light."

He seemed ready to spring.

I said quietly, "Will you be able to make executive decisions from cold storage? Scrutinize the links between economic growth and equity returns? Firm up the client franchise? Is China still outperforming India?"

He hit me, slammed the heel of his hand off my chest, and it hurt. The bench wobbled under my shifted weight. I got up and walked across the floor to the spare room, where I went directly to the window. Stood and looked. Spare land, skin and bones, distant ridges whose height I could not estimate without a dependable reference. Sky pale and bare, day fading in the west, if it was the west, if it was the sky.

I stepped back gradually and watched the view reduce itself within the limits of the window frame. Then I looked at the window itself, tall and narrow, top-ended by an arch. A lancet window, I thought, recalling the term, and this brought me back to myself, to a diminished perspective, something steadfast, a word with a meaning.

The bed was unmade, clothing scattered, and I understood that this was where my father slept and would sleep again, one more night, tonight, except that he would not sleep. Artis was in the adjoining room and I walked in and paused and then approached the bed. I saw that she was awake. I said nothing and simply leaned forward. Then I waited for her to recognize me.

Moving her lips, three unspoken words.

Come with us.

It was a joke, a last loving joke, but her face showed no sign of a smile.

Ross was back to pacing, wall to wall, more slowly now. He wore his dark glasses, which meant he was now invisible, at least to me. I headed out the door. He did not remind me to be here, this room, first thing, first light.

Love for a woman, yes. But I recalled what the Stenmark twins had said in the stone room, speaking directly to the wealthy benefactors. Take the leap, they said. Live the billionaire's myth of immortality. And why not now, I thought. What else was there for Ross to acquire? Give the futurists their blood money and they will make it possible for you to live forever.

The pod would be his final shrine of entitlement.

- 9 -

I knocked on a door and waited. I went to the next door and knocked and waited. Then I went down the hall knocking on doors and not waiting. It occurred to me that I'd done this two or three days earlier, or maybe it was two or three years. I walked and knocked and looked back eventually to see if any doors had opened. I imagined a telephone ringing on a desk behind one of the doors, ringer on Lo. I knocked on the door and reached for the doorknob, realizing there was no doorknob. I looked for a fixture on the door that might accommodate the disk on my wristband. I went down the hall and turned the corner and checked every door, knocking first and then searching for a magnetic component. The doors were painted in various pastels. I stood back against the opposite wall, where there were no doors, and scanned the doors that faced me, ten or eleven doors, and saw that none exactly matched another. This was art that belongs to the afterlife. It was art that accompanies last things, simple, dreamlike and delirious. You're dead, it said. I went down the hall and turned the corner and knocked on the first door.

In my room I tried to think about the matter. Ross could

not be the only one here who was ready to enter the chamber well before the body failed. Were these people deranged or were they in the forefront of a new consciousness? I lay on the bed and looked at the ceiling. The father-son exchange should have been more measured considering the nature of the revelation. I'd said foolish and indefensible things. In the morning I would talk to Ross and then remain at his side as he and Artis were taken down.

I slept a while and then went to the food unit. Empty, odorless, Monkless, no food in the slot, late for lunch, early for dinner, but do they observe these conventions?

I didn't want to go back to my room. Bed, chair, wall, so on, so on, so on.

Come with us, she said.

Fires were burning onscreen and a fleet of air tankers hung a thick haze of chemicals over the scorched treetops.

Then a single figure walking through a town's empty streets with homes imploded by heat and flame and lawn ornaments shriveled to a crisp.

Then a satellite image of twin lines of white smoke snaking across a gray landscape.

Elsewhere now people wearing facemasks, hundreds moving at camera level, walking or being carried by others, and was this a disease, a virus, long ranks of slow-moving men and women, and is it something spread by insects or vermin and carried on airborne dust, dead-eyed individuals, in the thousands now, walking at a stricken pace that resembled forever.

Then a woman seated on the roof of her car, head in hands, flames—the fire again—moving down the foothills in the near distance.

Then grass fires sweeping across the flatlands and a herd of bison, silhouetted in bright flame, going at a gallop parallel to barbed-wire fencing and out of the frame.

There was a quick cut to enormous ocean waves approaching and then water surging over seawalls and sets of imagery merging, skillfully edited but hard to absorb, towers shaking, a bridge collapsing, a tremendous close-up view of ash and lava blasting out of an opening in the earth's crust and I wanted it to last longer, it was right here, just above me, lava, magma, molten rock, but a few seconds later a dried lakebed appeared with one bent tree trunk standing and then back to wildfires in forested land and in open country and sweeping down into town and onto highways.

Then long views of wooded hillsides being swallowed in rolling smoke and a crew of firefighters in helmets and backpacks vanishing up a mountain trail and reappearing in a forest of splintered pines and bared bronze earth.

Then, up close, screen about to burst with flames that jump a stream and appear to spring into the camera and out toward the hallway where I stand watching.

I walked randomly for a time, seeing a woman open a door and enter whatever kind of space was situated there. I followed a work crew for fifty meters before I detoured into a corridor and went down a long ramp toward a door that had a doorknob. I hesitated, mind blank, and then turned the knob and pushed open the door and walked into earth, air and sky.

Here was a walled garden, trees, shrubs, flowering plants. I stood and looked. The heat was less severe than it had been on the day I'd arrived. This is what I needed, away from the rooms, the halls, the units—a place outside where I might think calmly about what I would see and hear and feel in the scene to come, at first light, when Artis and Ross were taken down. I walked for half a minute along a winding stone path before I realized, dumbly, that this was not a desert oasis but a proper English garden with trimmed hedges, shade trees, wild roses climbing a trellis. Something even stranger then, tree bark, blades of grass, every sort of flower—all seemingly coated or enameled, bearing a faint glaze. None of this was natural, all of it unruffled by the breeze that swept across the garden.

Trees and plants were labeled and I read some of the Latin names, which only deepened the mystery or the paradox or the ruse, whatever it was. It was the Stenmark twins, that's what it was. *Carpinus betulus fastigiata*, a pyramidal tree, green foliage, narrow trunk that felt clean and smooth to the touch, some kind of plastic or fiberglass, museum quality, and I kept checking labels, could not seem to stop, fragments of Latin sideswiping and intermingling, *Helianthus decapetalus*, tapered leaves, whorl of bright yellow petals, then a bench in the shadow of a tall oak and a still figure seated there, apparently human, in a loose gray shirt, gray trousers and silver skullcap. He turned my way and nodded, a gesture of permission, and I approached slowly. He was a man of considerable age, lean, with buttery brown skin, a pointed face and slender hands, neck tendons like bridge cables.

"You're the son," he said.

"I guess so, yes."

"I wonder how you managed to avoid the usual safeguards, making your way here."

"I think my disk malfunctioned. My wrist ornament."

"Magically," he said. "And there's a breeze this evening. Also magical."

He invited me to share the bench, which resembled a foreshortened church pew. His name was Ben-Ezra and he liked to come out here, he said, and think about the time, many years away, when he would return to the garden and sit on the same bench, reborn, and think about the time when he used to sit here, usually alone, and imagine that very moment.

"Same trees, same ivy."

"So I expect," he said.

"Or something completely different."

"What is here now is what is completely different. This is the lunar afterlife of the planet. Fabricated materials, a survival garden. It has its particular link to a life that is no longer in transit."

"Doesn't the garden also suggest a kind of mockery? Or is it a kind of nostalgia?"

"Much too soon for you to shake free of the conventions that you've brought here with you."

"And Ross, what about him?"

"Ross was quick to gain a secure understanding."

"And now here I am, faced with the death of a woman I admire and the rashly premature death of the man she loves, who happens to be my father. And what am I doing? I'm sitting on a bench in an English garden in the middle of a desert waste."

"We have not encouraged his plan."

"But you will allow him to do it. You will allow your team to do it."

"People who spend time here find out eventually who they are. Not through consultation with others but through self-examination, self-revelation. A tract of lost land, a sense of wilderness that is overwhelming. These rooms and halls, a stillness, a state of waiting. Aren't all of us here waiting for something to happen? Something elsewhere that will further define our purpose here. And something far more intimate as well. Waiting to enter the chamber, waiting to learn what we will confront there. A few of those waiting are fairly healthy, yes, very few, but they've chosen to surrender what is left of their current lives to discover a radical level of self-renewal."

"Ross has always been a master of life expectancy," I said. "Then, here, now, in the past three or four days, I'm seeing the man disintegrate."

"Another state of waiting. Waiting to decide finally. He has the rest of this day and a long sleepless night in which to think more deeply into the matter. And if he needs more time, this will be arranged."

"But in simple human terms, the man believes that he can't live without the woman."

"Then you are the one to tell him that what remains is worth a change of mind and heart."

"What is it that remains? Investment strategies?"

"The son remains."

"That won't work," I said.

"The son and what he might do to keep the father intact in the big bad world."

His voice had a slight lilt that he tended to accompany with a sway of index and middle fingers. I confronted the impulse to guess the man's background or to invent it. The name Ben-Ezra was itself an invention, so I decided. The name suited the man, suggesting a composite of biblical and futuristic themes, and here we were in his post-apocalyptic garden. I was sorry he'd told me his name, sorry he'd named himself before I could do it for him.

He wasn't done with fathers and sons.

"Allow the man the dignity of his choice. Forget his money. He has a life outside the limits of your experience. Grant him the right to his sorrow."

"His sorrow, yes. His choice, no. And the fact that this is allowable here, this is part of the program."

"Here and elsewhere, years to come, not uncommon."

We sat for a time without speaking. He wore dark slippers with tiny bright markings on each instep. I began to ask questions about the Convergence. He gave no direct responses but remarked along the way that the community was still growing, positions to be filled, construction projects to be initiated, subsurface. The airstrip, however, would remain a simple component, without expansion or modernization.

He said, "Isolation is not a drawback to those who understand that isolation is the point."

I tried to imagine him in ordinary surroundings, in the rear seat of a car moving slowly through crowded streets or at the head of a dinner table in his home on a hilltop above the crowded streets, but the idea carried no conviction. I could see him nowhere but here, on this bench, in the context of an immense emptiness outside the garden walls. He was indigenous. Isolation was the point.

"We understand that the idea of life extension will generate methods that attempt to improve upon the freezing of human bodies. To re-engineer the aging process, to reverse the biochemistry of progressive diseases. We fully expect to be in the forefront of any genuine innovation. Our tech centers in Europe are examining strategies for change. Ideas adaptable to our format. We're getting ahead of ourselves. This is where we want to be."

Did such a man have a family? Did he brush his teeth, see a dentist when he had a toothache? Could I even try to imagine his life? Someone else's life. Not even a minute. Even a minute is unimaginable. Physical, mental, spiritual. Not even the merest second. Too much is pledged into his compact frame.

I told myself to calm down.

He said, "How fragile we are. Isn't it true? Everyone everywhere on this earth."

I listened to him speak about the hundreds of millions of people into the future billions who are struggling to find something to eat not once or twice a day but all day every day. He spoke in detail about food systems, weather systems, the loss of forests, the spread of drought, the massive die-offs of birds and ocean life, the levels of carbon dioxide, the lack of drinking water, the waves of virus that envelop broad geographies.

These elements of planetary woe were a natural component of the thinking here but there was no trace of rote rec-
itation. He knew about these matters, he'd studied them,
witnessed some aspects of them, dreamt about them. And he
spoke in a subdued tone that carried an eloquence I could
not help admiring.

Then there was biological warfare with its variant forms of
mass extinction. Toxins, agents, replicating entities. And the
refugees everywhere, victims of war in great numbers, living
in makeshift shelters, unable to return to their crushed cities
and towns, dying at sea when their rescue vessels capsize.

He was looking at me, probing for something.

"Don't you see and feel these things more acutely than
you used to? The perils and warnings? Something gathering, no matter how safe you may feel in your wearable technology. All the voice commands and hyper-connections that
allow you to become disembodied."

I told him that what was gathering could well be a kind of
psychological pandemic. The fearful perception that tends
toward wishfulness. Something people want and need from
time to time, purely atmospheric.

I liked that. Purely atmospheric.

He looked at me even more searchingly now, either considering the remark too witless to address or interpreting
what I said as a gesture toward social convention, obligatory
under the circumstances.

"Atmospheric, yes. One minute, calm prevails. Then there's
a light in the sky and a sonic boom and a shock wave—and a
Russian city enters a compressed reality that would be mys-
tifying if it weren't so abruptly real. This is nature's thrust,

its command over our efforts, our foresight, every ingenuity we can summon to protect ourselves. The meteor. Chelyabinsk."

He smiled at me.

"Say it. Go ahead. Chelyabinsk," he said. "Not so very far from here. Quite near in fact, if anything can be called near in this part of the world. People rush from room to room collecting valuable documents. They prepare to go somewhere that's safe. They put their cats and dogs in carriers."

He stopped and thought.

"We reverse the text here, we read the news backwards. From death to life," he said. "Our devices enter the body dynamically and become the refurbished parts and pathways we need in order to live again."

"Is the desert where miracles happen? Are we here to repeat the ancient pieties and superstitions?"

It amused him to hear that I was not inclined to yield.

"Such a quaint response to ideas that attempt to confront a decimated future. Try to understand. This is all happening in the future. This future, this instant. If you can't absorb this idea, best go home now."

I wondered whether Ross had asked this man to speak to me, enlighten me, expertly, reassuringly. Was I interested in what he had to say? I found myself thinking of the dire night ahead and the morning to come.

"We share a feeling here, a perception. We think of ourselves as transrational. The location itself, the structure itself, the science that bends all previous belief. The testing of human viability."

He paused here to remove a handkerchief from his trouser pocket and blow his nose, unconditionally, with follow-up swipes and blots, and this made me feel better. Real life, body functions. I waited for him to finish what he was saying.

"Those of us who are here don't belong anywhere else. We've fallen out of history. We've abandoned who we were and where we were in order to be here."

He inspected the handkerchief and folded it carefully. It took him a moment to ease the small square into his pocket.

"And where is here?" he said. "Untapped reserves of rare minerals and the rolling thunder of oil money and repressive states and human rights violations and bribable officials. Minimal contact. Detachment. Disinfestation."

I wanted to interpret the marks imprinted on his slippers. These might be a clue to the man's cultural lineage. I got nowhere with this, feeling the breeze begin to stiffen and hearing the voice once more.

"The site is fixed. We are not in a zone susceptible to earthquakes or to minor swarms but there are seismic countermeasures in every detail of the structure, with every conceivable safeguard against systems failure. Artis will be safe, and Ross if he chooses to accompany her. The site is fixed, we are fixed."

Ben-Ezra. I needed to think about his real name, his birth name. I needed a form of self-defense, a way to creep insidiously into his life. I'd want to give him a cane to complete the picture, a walking stick, rock maple, man on the bench, both hands resting on the curved handle, shaft perpendicular to the ground, blunt end between his feet.

"Those who eventually emerge from the capsules will be

ahistorical humans. They will be free of the flatlines of the past, the attenuated minute and hour."

"And they will speak a new language, according to Ross."

"A language isolate, beyond all affiliation with other languages," he said. "To be taught to some, implanted in others, those already in cryopreservation."

A system that will offer new meanings, entire new levels of perception.

It will expand our reality, deepen the reach of our intellect.

It will remake us, he said.

We will know ourselves as never before, blood, brain and skin.

We will approximate the logic and beauty of pure mathematics in everyday speech.

No similes, metaphors, analogies.

A language that will not shrink from whatever forms of objective truth we have never before experienced.

He talked, I listened, the subject beginning to approach new magnitudes.

The universe, what it was, what it is, where it is going.

The expanding, accelerating, infinitely evolving universe, so filled with life, with worlds upon never-ending worlds, he said.

The universe, the multiverse, so many cosmic infinities that the idea of repeatability becomes unavoidable.

The idea of two individuals sitting on a bench in a desert garden having the conversation we are having, you and I, word for word, except that they are different individuals, in a different garden, millions of light-years from here—this is an inescapable fact.

Was this the case of an old man getting carried away or was it the younger man's attempt to resist slick ironies that mattered?

Either way I began to think of him as a crackpot sage.

"It's only human to want to know more, and then more, and then more," I said. "But it's also true that what we don't know is what makes us human. And there's no end to not knowing."

"Go on."

"And no end to not living forever."

"Go on," he said.

"If someone or something has no beginning, then I can believe that he, she or it has no end. But if you're born or hatched or sprouted, then your days are already numbered."

He thought for a moment.

"'It is the heaviest stone that melancholy can throw at a man to tell him that he is at the end of his nature, or that there is no further state to come.'"

I waited.

"Seventeenth century," he said. "Sir Thomas Browne."

I waited some more. But that was all. Seventeenth century. He left it up to me to reckon our progress since then.

True wind blowing now, garden unstirred, the eerie stillness of flowers, grass and leaves that resist the perceptible rush of air. But the scene is not blandly static. There is tone and color, shimmer everywhere, sun beginning to sink, trees alight in the span of waning day.

"You sit alone in a quiet room at home and you listen carefully. What is it you hear? Not traffic in the street, not voices or rain or someone's radio," he said. "You hear something but what? It's not room tone or ambient sound. It's something that may change as your listening deepens, second after second, and the sound is growing louder now — not louder but somehow wider, sustaining itself, encircling itself. What is it? The mind, the life itself, your life? Or is it the world, not the material mass, land and sea, but what inhabits the world, the flood of human existence. The world hum. Do you hear it, yourself, ever?"

I could not invent a name for him. I could not imagine him as a younger man. He was born old. He has lived his life on this bench. He is a permanent part of the bench, Ben-Ezra, slippers, skullcap, long spidery fingers, a body at rest in a spun-glass garden.

I left him there and began to wander out past the flower-beds, on a dirt path now, pushing through a gated part of the garden wall into deeper stands of counterfeit trees. Then something stopped me cold, a figure standing in scant light, nearly inseparable from the trees, face and body scorched brown, arms crossed on chest, fists clenched, and even when I knew that I was staring at a mannequin, I remained in place, rooted as the figure itself.

It scared me, a thing without features, naked, sexless, no longer a dummy dress-form but a sentinel, posing forbiddingly. This was different from the mannequin I'd seen in an empty hallway. There was a tension in this encounter and I walked on warily and saw several others, half hidden in the trees. I didn't look at them so much as watch them, scrutinize them nervously. Their stillness seemed willed. They stood with arms crossed or arms at sides or arms thrust forward, one of them armless, one of them headless, strong dumb-struck objects that belonged here, painted in dark washes.

In a small clearing there was a structure jutting upward at a slant from ground level, a rooflike projection above an entranceway. I walked down eight or nine steps into a vaulted interior, a crypt, dimly lit, dank, all cracked gray stone, with recesses in the walls where bodies were placed, half bodies, mannequins as preserved corpses, head to waist in shabby hooded garments, each to its niche.

I stood there and tried to absorb what I was seeing. I searched for the word. There was a word I wanted, not *crypt* or *grotto*, and in the meantime all I could do was look intently and try to accumulate the details. These mannequins had features, all worn down, eroded, eyes, nose, mouth, ruined faces every one, ash gray, and shriveled hands, barely intact. There were roughly twenty such figures and a few that were full-bodied, standing, in old gray shredded robes, heads bowed. I walked along, bodies on both sides of me, and the sight was overwhelming, and the place itself, the word itself—the word was *catacomb*.

These figures, these desert saints, mummified, desiccated in their underground burial chamber, the claustrophobic power of the scene, the faint stink of rot. I was breathless for a moment. Could I avoid interpreting the figures as an ancestral version of the upright men and women in their cryonic capsules, actual humans on the verge of immortal-ity? I didn't want interpretation. I wanted to see and feel what was here, even if I was unequal to the experience as it folded over me.

How could it be that mannequins had this effect, deeper even than the sight of embalmed human beings centuries old in a church or monastery? I'd never been to such a site, to a charnel house in Italy or France, but I could not imagine a stronger response. What was I seeing in this hole in the ground? Not sculpted marble or a delicate strip of pinewood hand-carved with a chisel and highlighted in gold leaf. These were pieces of plastic, synthetic compounds draped in dead men's hoods and robes, and they brought a faint yearning to the scene, the illusion of humanoid aspiration. But I was interpreting again, wasn't I? Feeling hungry and weak and so scraped raw by the day's events that I expected statues to speak.

Farther along, beyond the two rows of bodies, there was a floating white light and I needed to put a hand to my face when I drew near, deflecting the glare. Here were figures submerged in a pit, mannequins in convoluted mass, naked, arms jutting, heads horribly twisted, bare skulls, an entanglement of tumbled forms with jointed limbs and bodies, neutered humans, men and women stripped of identity, faces blank except for one unpigmented figure, albino, staring at me, pink eyes flashing.

In the food unit I put my face nearly into the plate and chewed the last few bites of dinner. All the food units throughout the complex, one person in each, stacked in my mind. I went to my room, turned on the light and sat in the chair thinking. It felt as though I'd done this a thousand times, same room every time, same person in the chair. I found myself listening. I tried to empty my mind and simply listen. I wanted to hear what Ben-Ezra had described, the oceanic sound of people living and thinking and talking, billions, everywhere, waiting for trains, marching to war, licking food off their fingers. Or simply being who they are.

The world hum.

- 10 -

I need to come at this in the simplest way.

He sits staring into the wall, a man unreachably apart. He is already locked in retrospection, seeing Artis, I thought, in drifting images, something he can't control, flaring memories, apparitions, all set in motion by the fact of his decision.

He will not be going with her.

It was pounding him down, everything, the stone weight of a lifetime, everything he'd ever said and done brought to this moment. Here he is, wan and slack, hair mussed, tie unknotted, hands loosely folded at his crotch. I stand nearby, not knowing how to stand, how to adjust to the occasion, but determined to watch him openly. His eyes are empty of any plea he might make for understanding. How things change overnight, and what was hard and fast becomes some limp witness to a man's wavering heart, and where the man had spoken forcefully the day before, striding wall to wall, he now sits slumped, thinking of the woman he has abandoned.

He'd told me his decision in the barest words. It was a sound straight from nature, unprocessed, without expressive affect. He didn't have to tell me that Artis had already been taken down. It was in his voice. There was just the room, the chair, the man in the chair. There was the awkward watchful son. There were the two escorts flanking the doorway.

I waited for someone to make the first move. Then I did, shifting slightly into a more or less formal mourner's pose, conscious that I'd been wearing the same stale shirt and pants since my arrival here, with underwear and socks I'd scrubbed at dawn, using hand sanitizer.

Soon Ross got out of the chair and moved toward the door and I followed closely, neither of us speaking, my hand in contact with his elbow, not guiding or supporting but only offering the comfort of touch.

Is a man of epic wealth allowed to be broken by grief?

The escorts were women, one holstered, the younger not. They led us to a space that became an abstract thing, a theoretical occurrence. I don't know how else to put it. An idea of motion that was also a change of position or place. This was not the first such experience I'd had here, four of us this time observing a silence that felt reverent. I wasn't sure whether this was due to the sad circumstances or to the nature of the conveyance, the feel of angled descent, the feel of being detached from our sensory apparatus, coasting in a way that was mental more than physical.

I decided to test the setting, to say something, anything.

"What's it called, this thing we're in?"

I was pretty sure I'd spoken but could not determine whether my words had produced a sound. I looked at the escorts.

Then Ross said, "It's called the veer."

"The veer," I said.

I put a hand on his shoulder, pressed down, gripped hard, letting him know that I was here, we were both here.

"The veer," I said again.

I was always repeating things here, I was verifying, trying to establish secure placement. Artis was down there somewhere, at veer's end, counting drops of water on a shower curtain.

I stood watching through a narrow glass panel, eye-high. This was my role here, to watch whatever they put in front of me. The team in Zero K was preparing Artis for cryopreservation, doctors and others dressed variously, some in motion, others scanning monitors, adjusting equipment.

Artis was somewhere in their midst, sheeted, on a table. She was visible only momentarily, in fragments, mid-body, lower legs, never a clear view of the face. The team worked over and around her. I didn't know whether to regard the physical form they were working on as "the body." Maybe she was still alive. Maybe this was the moment, the second, in which she was being chemically induced to expire.

The other thing I didn't know was what constituted the end. When does the person become the body? There were levels of surrender, I thought. The body withdraws from one function and then possibly another, or possibly not—heart, nervous system, brain, different parts of the brain down into the mechanism of individual cells. It occurred to me that there was more than one official definition, none characterized by unanimous assent. They made it up as the occasion required. Doctors, lawyers, theologians, philosophers, professors of ethics, judges and juries.

It also occurred to me that my mind was wandering.

Think of Ross on the table if he'd so decided, healthy man in systemic collapse. He was in the anteroom, waiting out the time. I was the sole willing witness, and now her face, a touching glimpse, Artis, team members swinging past in their caps, scrubs, masks, surgical gowns, tunic tops, lab coats.

Then the viewing slot went blank.

A guide with dreadlocks led us to a site, saying nothing, letting us absorb what we were seeing.

Ross asked a question now and then. He had combed his hair, knotted his tie and adjusted the trim of his suit jacket. The voice was not quite his but he was talking, trying to place himself in the midst of things.

We stood in the aisle above a small sloped gallery and looked at three human figures in a plain space so deftly lit that the outer margins dissolved in shadow. These were individuals in clear casings, in body pods, and they were naked, one man, two women, shaved heads, all three.

Tableau vivant, I thought, except that the actors were dead and their costumes were super-insulated plastic tubes.

The guide told us that these people were among those who had chosen to be taken early. Perhaps they had five or ten years remaining, or twenty, or more. They'd been stripped of their essential organs, which were being preserved separately, brains included, in insulated vessels called organ pods.

"They seem at peace," Ross said.

The bodies were not formally posed. Eyes were open in glazed wonder, arms loosely at sides, knees naturally knobbed and furrowed, no hair anywhere.

"They're just standing and waiting," he said. "All the time in the world."

He was thinking of Artis, what else, wondering what she was feeling, if anything, and which stage she had reached in the body-cooling process.

Vitrification, cryopreservation, nanotechnology.

Cherish the language, I thought. Let the language reflect the search for ever more obscure methods, down into subatomic levels.

The guide spoke with an accent I took to be Russian. She wore sleek jeans and a long fringed shirt and I tried to convince myself that she was posed in a manner identical to that of the bodies. This was not true but it took me a while to abandon the idea.

Ross kept looking. These were lives in abeyance. Or the empty framework of lives beyond retrieval. And the man himself, my father. I wondered how his change-of-mind would affect his honorary status here, the thrust of executive command. I knew what I was feeling, a sympathy bled white by disappointment. The man had backed down.

He spoke to the guide without taking his eyes off the figures standing before us.

"What do you call them?"

"We are told to call them heralds."

"Makes sense," he said.

"Showing the way, making the path."

"Being early, being first," he said.

"They do not wait."

"They do it before they have to do it."

"Heralds," she said.

"They look serene."

Thinking of Artis, seeing her, determined to go with her. But he had backed down. The idea of joining her had been driven by some deranged tide of love. But once sworn to the act, he needed to be true to it. The full swing of life and career, man at the center of money's magnetic field. Okay, I'm making too much of his reputation and material worth. But this is a component of the outsized life. Too much engenders too much.

He took a seat in the last row and after a while I joined him. Then I looked at the bodies.

There was the question of who they were, everything that had gone before, the inexpressibly dense experience of a man or woman alive on the earth. Here, they were laboratory life-forms shaved naked in pods and drawn together as one unit whatever the means of canning and curing. And they were located in a space that was anonymous, no where or when, a tactic that matched every aspect of my experience here.

The guide explained the meaning of the term Zero K. This was rote narration, with plotted stops and restarts, and it concerned a unit of temperature called absolute zero, which is minus two hundred and seventy-three point one five degrees celsius. A physicist named Kelvin was mentioned, he was the K in the term. The most interesting thing the guide had to say was the fact that the temperature employed in cryostorage does not actually approach zero K.

The term, then, was pure drama, another stray trace of the Stenmark twins.

"We'll leave together. We'll pack and leave," Ross said.

"I've been packed since I arrived."

"Good."

"There's nothing to pack."

"Good. We'll leave together," he said again.

These were the commonplace words, the sounds he needed to make in order to restore a sense of function. I had a feeling there was more to come, possibly not so reassuring to either one of us.

"I told myself finally, dead of night, that I had a responsibility to keep living. Suffer the loss, live and suffer and hope it gets easier—not easier but so deeply embedded, the loss, the absence, that I can carry it. To go with her would have been the wrong kind of surrender. I had no right. It was an abuse of privilege. What did you say to me when we argued?"

"I don't know."

"You said if I went with her, it would reduce you. My over-dominance, the thing you can't escape. Even loving her too much, even choosing to die too soon. It would have been the kind of surrender in which I gain control instead of relinquishing it."

I studied body color. Woman, man, woman. The range was narrow but is it possible to be precise about skin color in any situation? Yellow brown black white, all wrong except as convenient labels. Did I want to resort to nuances of tone, to amber, umber, lunar? When I was fourteen I would have died trying.

"In the end what did I do? I tried to face it," he said. "And this meant I had to tell her. I sat next to the bed in the dim room. Did she understand what I was saying? Did she hear me at all? I wasn't sure. Did she forgive me? I kept asking her to forgive me. Then I rambled, on and on. Did I need a response? Did I fear a response? *Forgive me. Wait for me. I will join you soon.* On and on, whispering. I thought maybe she can hear me if I whisper."

"She may have been alive but she was beyond any kind of contact."

"Then I just sat there until they came to take her down."

Some sag here and there, completely normal, in chest, breasts and bellies. Look long enough and even the shaved heads of the women begin to seem consistent with the primal chill of nature. This was a function of the pods, I thought, the detailed rigor of scientific method, humans stripped of adornment, spliced back to fetushood.

The guide said there was something else we might find interesting to look at.

How many days now, how many interesting things to look at? The screens, the catacombs, the skull on the wall in the stone room. They were drenching me in last things. I thought about these two words. This is eschatology, isn't it? Not just the damped echo of a life that slides away but words with all-encompassing impact, beyond appeals to reason. *Last Things.* I told myself to stop.

Ross lowered his head, closed his eyes.

Thinking of Artis. I imagined him at home, sitting in his study with a whiskey in hand, hearing himself breathe. The time he'd visited her on a dig somewhere at desert's edge outside a Bedouin village. I try to see what he sees but can only imagine her in another desert, this one, in whole-body suspension, eyes closed, head shaved, a sliver of mind still intact. He has to believe this—memories ingrained in brain tissue.

Departure time soon. Armored car waiting, smoked windows, driver with sidearm. An overtone of protection that makes me feel small, weak and threatened.

But was it simply love that made him want to join her? Maybe I preferred to think that he was driven by a dark yearning, a need to be deprived of what he is and what he possesses, stripped of everything, hollowed out, organs stored, body propped alongside others in a colony of pods. It is the same undercurrent of self-repudiation that made him change his name, only deeper and stronger. A dark yearning, I liked that. But what was my point? Why did I want to imagine such a thing about my father? Because this place is drenching me in bad blood. And because this is the song-and-dance version of what happens to self-made men. They unmake themselves.

When he joins her, in three years or thirteen, will nano-technologists steer their ages downward? And on being revived, whenever that is, the first moment of their earthly afterlife, will Artis be twenty-five years old, twenty-seven, Ross thirty or thirty-one? Think of the soulful reunion. Let's have a baby. And where will I be, how old and begrudging and piss-stained, how spooked to be embracing my spirited

young father and newborn half-brother, who has my withered finger gripped in his tiny trembling hand.

Nanobots—a child's word.

I kept looking straight ahead, looking and thinking. The
fact that these individuals, these heralds, had chosen to be
rendered dead well before their time. The fact that their
bodies had been emptied of indispensable organs. The fact
of containment, alignment, bodies set in assigned positions.
Woman man woman. It occurred to me that these were
humans as mannequins. I allowed myself to think of them
as brainless objects playing out a reversal of the spectacle
I'd encountered earlier—the mannequins hunched in their
burial chamber, in hoods and robes. And now this freeze-
frame of naked humans in pods.

The guide told us again that there was another area of
possible interest.

I wanted to see beauty in these stilled figures, an imposing design not of clockwork bodies but of the simple human
structure and its extensions, inward and out, each individual implacably unique in touch, taste and spirit. There they
stand, not trying to tell us something but suggesting none-
theless the mingled astonishments of our lives, here, on
earth.

Instead I wondered if I was looking at the controlled
future, men and women being subordinated, willingly or
not, to some form of centralized command. Mannequined
lives. Was this a facile idea? I thought about local matters,
the disk on my wristband that tells them, in theory, where I
am at all times. I thought about my room, small and tight but
embodying an odd totalness. Other things here, the halls,

the veers, the fabricated garden, the food units, the unidentifiable food, or when does utilitarian become totalitarian.

Was there a hollowness in these notions? Maybe they were nothing more than an indication of my eagerness to get home. Do I remember where I live? Do I still have a job? Can I still bum a cigarette from a girlfriend after a movie?

The guide had told us about brains preserved in insulated vessels. Now she added that heads, entire heads with brains intact, were sometimes removed from the bodies and stored separately. One day in decades to come the head will be grafted to a healthy nanobody.

And would all the revivified lives be identical, trimmed tight by the process itself? Die a human, be reborn an isometric drone.

I nudged my father and said quietly, "Do they ever get a hard-on, dead men in pods? Jolted by some malfunction, a shift in temperature levels that creates a kind of *zing* running through the body and causing their dicks to spring up, all the men at once, in all the pods."

"Ask the guide," he said.

I gave him a backhand tap on the arm and we got up and followed the woman down a corridor that tapered to the degree that we had to proceed, finally, single-file. Sound began to pale, our footsteps fading, the brush-touch of our bodies against the confining walls.

There is one thing more, something interesting, the guide had said.

We stood in the entranceway of a large white room. The walls did not have the same rough surface I'd seen elsewhere. This was hard smooth rock and Ross put his hand to the wall and said that it was fine-grained white marble. He knew this, I did not. The room was stone cold and, at first, in every direction, it was all the same, nothing but walls, floor and ceiling. I spread my arms in a dumb dramatic gesture to render the size of the grand space but restrained myself from trying to estimate length, width and height.

I moved forward, briefly, and Ross followed. I looked past him to the guide, waiting for her to say something, give us some clue to the nature of the site. Was it a site or just an idea for a site? My father and I studied the room together. I tried to imagine what I was seeing even as I saw it. What made the experience so elusive? A large room, a couple of men standing and looking. A woman at the entrance, dead still. An art gallery, I thought, with nothing in it. The gallery is the art, the space itself, the walls and floor. Or an enormous marble tomb, a mass gravesite emptied of bodies or waiting for bodies. No ornamental cornice or frieze, just flat walls of shiny white marble.

I looked at Ross, who was staring past me toward a far corner of the room. It took me a moment, everything here took me a moment. Then I saw what he saw, a figure seated on the floor near the junction of the two walls. Small human figure, motionless, seeping gradually into my level of awareness. I had to tell myself that I was not somewhere else trying to visualize what I was actually seeing, here and now, in solid form.

My father walked in that direction, hesitantly, and I followed, walking and pausing. The seated figure was a girl, barefoot, legs crossed. She wore loose white pants and a white knee-length blouse. One arm was raised and bent toward the body at neck level. The other arm was waist-high at a matching angle.

We stopped walking, Ross and I. We were still some distance from the figure but it seemed an intrusion, a violation, to move any closer. Hair trimmed in a mannish cut, head bowed slightly, feet positioned with bottoms turned upward.

Was I sure that it was not a boy?

Her eyes were closed. I knew that her eyes were closed even if this was not evident from where we stood. Her youth was not necessarily evident but I felt free to believe that she was young. She had to be young. And she had no nationality. She had to be nationless.

A chill white silence everywhere in the room. Did I fold my arms across my chest to contain my response to the beauty of the scene, or was I just cold?

We backed away then, slightly, simultaneously. Even if I knew the reason for her presence and her pose, it would defy all meaning. Meaning was exhausted in the figure itself, the sight itself.

"Artis would know how to interpret this," Ross said.

"And I would ask her whether it's a boy or girl."

"And she would say what's the difference."

The fact of life, one small body with beating heart in this soaring mausoleum, and she would be here long after we were gone, day and night, I knew this, a space conceived and designed for a figure in stillness.

Before we left the area I turned to take one last look and, yes, she was there, in empty method, a living breathing artform, boy or girl, seated in pajamalike garments, offering nothing more for me to think or imagine. The guide led us down a long hall that was not bordered by doors and Ross began to speak to me now, a faraway voice, close to the trembling bend.

"People getting older become more fond of objects. I think this is true. Particular things. A leather-bound book, a piece of furniture, a photograph, a painting, the frame that holds the painting. These things make the past seem permanent. A baseball signed by a famous player, long dead. A simple coffee mug. Things we trust. They tell an important story. A person's life, all those who entered and left, there's a depth, a richness. We used to sit in a certain room, often, the room with the monochrome paintings. She and I. The room in the townhouse with those five paintings and the tickets we saved and framed, like a couple of teenage tourists, two tickets to a bullfight in Madrid. She was already in poor condition. We didn't say much. Just sat there remembering."

There were long pauses between sentences and his tone was near to a murmur, or an underbreath, and I listened hard and waited.

Then I said, "What is the fond object in your case?"

"I don't know yet. Maybe I'll never know."

"Not the paintings."

"Too many. Too much."

"The tickets. Two small slips of paper."

"Sol y sombra. Plaza de Toros Las Ventas," he said. "We were seated in an area that's sometimes in the sun, sometimes in the shade. Open area. Sol y sombra."

He wasn't finished, a man propelled into obsessive reflection. He talked, I listened, his voice more halting, the subject more elusive. Did I want to stare at the guide and try to think of us together in a room, my room, she and I, the guide, the escort, or just visualize her alone, nowhere, a woman stepping out of her shoes. I felt an erotic wistfulness but could not shape it.

We stood in the veer, gliding out of Zero K, out of the numbered levels. I thought of prime numbers. I thought, Define a prime. The veer was an environment, I thought, suited to rigorous thinking. I was always good at math. I felt sure of myself when I dealt with numbers. Numbers were the language of science. And now I needed to find the precise and perpetual and more or less mandatory wording that would constitute the definition of a prime. But why did I need to do this? The guide stood with eyes closed, thinking in Russian. My father was in a waking state of mindlapse, in retreat from his pain. I thought, Prime number. A positive integer not divisible. But what was the rest of it? What else about primes? What else about integers?

I walked the halls toward the room, eager to grab my bag and meet my father and head home. This was the one energy left to me, the expectation of return. Sidewalks, streets, green light, red light, metered seconds to get to the other side alive.

But I had to pause now, stop and look, because the screen in the ceiling began to lower and a series of images filled the width of the hallway.

People running, crowds of running men and women, they're closely packed and showing desperation, dozens, then hundreds, workpants, T-shirts, sweatshirts, shouldering each other, elbowing, looking dead ahead, the camera positioned slightly above, an angled shot, no cuts, tilts, pans. I back away instinctively. There's no soundtrack but it's almost possible to hear the mass pulse of breath and pounding feet. They're running on a surface barely visible beneath their crowded bodies. I see tennis shoes, ankle boots, sandals, there's a barefoot woman, a man in sneakers with undone laces flapping.

They keep on coming, trying to escape some dreadful spectacle or rumbling threat. I'm watching closely and trying to think into the action onscreen, the uniformity of it, the orderly deployment and steady pace that underlie the urgent scene. It begins to occur to me that I may be seeing the same running cluster repeatedly, shot and reshot, two dozen runners made to resemble several hundred, a flawless sleight of editing.

Here they come, mouths open, arms pumping, headbands, visors, camouflage caps, no seeming slowdown, and then something further comes to mind. Is it possible that this is not factual documentation rendered in a selective manner but something radically apart? It's a digital weave, every fragment manipulated and enhanced, all of it designed, edited, redesigned. Why hadn't this occurred to me before, in earlier screenings, the monsoon rains, the tornadoes? These were visual fictions, the wildfires and burning monks, digital bits, digital code, all of it computer-generated, none of it real.

I watched until the images faded and the screen began to lift, soundlessly, and I'd gone only a short way along the hall when there was a noise, hard to identify and rapidly getting louder. I went a few more paces and had to stop, the noise nearly upon me, and then they came wheeling around the corner charging in my direction, the running men and women, images bodied out, spilled from the screen. I hurried to the only safety there was, the nearest wall, back flattened, arms spread, the runners bearing down, nine or ten abreast, blasting past, wild-eyed. I could see their sweat and smell their stink and they kept on coming, all looking directly ahead.

Be calm. See what's here. Think about it clearly.

A local ritual upheld, a marathon of sacred awe, some obscure tradition adhered to for a hundred years. This was all the time I had for theories. They approached and went past and I looked at the faces and then at the bodies and saw the man with flapping laces and tried to see the barefoot woman. How many runners, who were they, why were they being filmed, are they still being filmed? I watched them come and go and then, in the thinning lines, with the last runners approaching, what I saw was a pair of tall blondish men and I leaned forward for a better look as they went by, shoulder to shoulder, and it was the Stenmark twins, unmistakably, Lars and Nils, or Jan and Sven.

They were drenching me, out-thinking me, these several days, this extreme sublifetime. What was it beyond a concentrated lesson in bewilderment?

It was their game, their mob, and they were a sweating panting part of it. The Stenmarks. I kept to the wall, watching them blow past and go racing down the long hall. When the runners were gone I remained in position, wallbound for a moment more. Was I surprised to learn that I was the only witness to whatever it was I'd just seen?

An empty hall.

The fact is I did not expect to see others. It had never occurred to me that there were others in the hall. It was uncommon in my experience that there were such others, with several brief exceptions. I stood away from the wall now, mind and body buzzing and the hallway seeming to tremble with the muffled thrust of the runners.

On the way back to my room I realized that I was limping.

ARTIS MARTINEAU

But am I who I was.

I think I am someone. There is someone here and I feel it in me or with me.

But where is here and how long am I here and am I only what is here.

She knows these words. She is all words but she doesn't know how to get out of words into being someone, being the person who knows the words.

Time. I feel it in me everywhere. But I don't know what it is.

The only time I know is what I feel. It is all now. But I don't know what this means.

I hear words that are saying things to me again and again. Same words all the time going away and coming back.

But am I who I was.

She is trying to understand what has happened to her and where she is and what it means to be who she is.

What is it that I am waiting for.

Am I only here and now. What happened to me that did this.

She is first person and third person both.

The only here is where I am. But where is here. And why just here and nowhere else.

What I don't know is right here with me but how do I make myself know it.

Am I someone or is it just the words themselves that make me think I'm someone.

Why can't I know more. Why just this and nothing else. Or do I need to wait.

She is able to say what she feels and she is also the person who stands outside the feelings.

Are the words themselves all there is. Am I just the words.

This is the feeling I have that the words want to tell me things but I don't know how to listen.

I listen to what I hear.

I only hear what is me. I am made of words.

Does it keep going on like this.

Where am I. What is a place. I know the feeling of some-where but I don't know where it is.

What I understand comes from nowhere. I don't know what I understand until I say it.

I am trying to become someone.

The involutions, the mind drift.

I almost know some things. I think I am going to know things but then it does not happen.

I feel something outside me that belongs to me.

Where is my body. Do I know what this is. I only know the word and I know it out of nowhere.

I know that I am inside something. I am somebody inside this thing I am in.

Is this my body.

Is this what makes me whatever I know and whatever I am.

I am nowhere that I can know or feel.

I will try to wait.

Everything I don't know is right here with me but how do I make myself know it.

Am I someone or is it just the words themselves that make me think I'm someone.

Why can't I know more. Why just this and nothing else. Or do I need to wait.

She is living within the grim limits of self.

Are the words themselves all there is. Am I just the words.

Will I ever stop thinking. I need to know more but I also need to stop thinking.

I try to know who I am.

But am I who I was and do I know what this means.

She is first person and third person with no way to join them together.

What I need to do is stop this voice.

But then what happens. And how long am I here. And is this all the time or only the least time there is.

Is all the time still to come.

Can't I stop being who I am and become no one.

She is the residue, all that is left of an identity.

I listen to what I hear. I can only hear what is me.

I can feel time. I am all time. But I don't know what this means.

I am only what is here and now.

How much time am I here. Where is here.

I think that I can see what I am saying.

But am I who I was. And what does this mean. And did someone do something to me.

Is this the nightmare of self drawn so tight that she is trapped forever.

I try to know who I am.

But all I am is what I am saying and this is nearly nothing.

She is not able to see herself, give herself a name, estimate the time since she began to think what she is thinking.

I think I am someone. But I am only saying words.

The words never go away.

Minutes, hours, days and years. Or is everything she knows contained in one timeless second.

This is all so small. I think that I am barely here.

It is only when I say something that I know that I am here.

Do I need to wait.

Here and now. This is who I am but only this.

She tries to see words. Not the letters in the words but the words themselves.

What does it mean to touch. I can almost touch whatever is here with me.

Is this my body.

I think I am someone. What does it mean to be who I am.

All the selves an individual possesses. What is left to her but a voice in its barest sheddings.

I try to see the words. Same words all the time.

The words float past.

Am I just the words. I know that there is more.

Does she need third person. Let her live down in the soundings inside herself. Let her ask her questions to no one but herself.

But am I who I was.

On and on. Eyes closed. Woman's body in a pod.

PART TWO

In the Time
of Konstantinovka

- 1 -

The office belonged to a man named Silverstone. It was my father's former office and two of the paintings he owned were still on the wall, dark with strips of dusty sunlight, both of them. I had to force myself to look at Silverstone, behind the burnished desk, while he droned his way through a global roundup that ranged from Hungary to South Africa, the forint to the rand.

Ross had made a phone call on my behalf and even as I sat here I tried to feel the kind of separation, the lingering distance that had always defined the time I spent in an office, a man with a job, a position—not an occupation exactly but a rank, a role, a title.

This job would make me the Son. Word of the interview would spread and everyone here would think of me this way. The job was not an unconditional gift. I would have to earn the right to keep it but my father's name would haunt every step I took, every word I spoke.

Then, again, I already knew that I would turn down the offer, any offer, whatever the rank or role.

Silverstone was a broad and mostly bald man whose

hands were active elements in the monologue he was delivering and I found myself imitating his gestures in abridged form, an alternative to nodding or to muttering microdecibels of assent. We could have been a teacher and his student in some rendition of the manual alphabet.

The forint got a finger twirl, the rand earned a fist.

The two paintings were the spectral remains of my father's presence here. I thought about my last visit to the office and there was Ross standing by the window, at night, wearing sunglasses. This was before the journey he'd make with his wife and the journey home with his son, mostly bloated time since then, for me at least, two years of it, slow-going and unfocused.

Silverstone became more specific, telling me that I'd be part of a group involved in the infrastructure of water. This was a term I'd never heard before. He spoke of water stress and water conflict. He referred to maps of water risk that guided investors. There were charts, he said, detailing the intersection of capital and water technology.

The paintings on the wall were not watercolors but I decided not to point this out. No need for me to bare the shallower reaches of my disposition.

He would confer with my father and several others and then make the offer. I would wait several days, reminding myself that I needed a job badly, and then reject the offer, graciously, without further comment.

I listened to the man and occasionally spoke. I said smart things. I sounded smart to myself. But why was I here? Did I need to lie, in three dimensions, over a period of time, with hand gestures? Was I defying a persistent urge to submit to the pressures of reality? There was only one thing I knew for certain. I would do it this way because it made me more interesting. Does that sound crazy? It showed me who I was in ways I did not try to understand.

Ross was not part of my thinking here. He and I were determined not to end in willful bitterness and none of this maneuvering was directed at him. He'd probably be relieved when I turned down the offer.

All through the episode with Silverstone I saw myself seated here attending to the man's water talk. Who was more absurd, he or I?

In the evening I would describe the man to Emma, repeat what he'd said. This is something I did well, word for word at times, and I looked forward to a late dinner in a modest restaurant on a tree-lined street between the brawling traffic of the avenues, our mood nicely guided by the infrastructure of water.

When we returned from the Convergence I announced to Ross that we were back in history now. Days have names and numbers, a discernible sequence, and there is an aggregate of past events, both immediate and long gone, that we can attempt to understand. Certain things are predictable, even within the array of departures from the common order. Elevators go up and down rather than sideways. We see the people who serve the food we eat in public establishments. We walk on paved surfaces and stand on a corner to hail a cab. Taxicabs are yellow, fire trucks red, bikes mostly blue. I'm able to return to my devices, data roaming, instant by instant, in the numbing raptures of the Web.

It turned out that my father was not interested in history or technology or hailing a cab. He let his hair grow wild and walked nearly everywhere he cared to go, which was nearly nowhere. He was slow and a little stooped and when I spoke about exercise, diet and self-responsibility, we both understood that this was just an inventory of hollow sounds.

His hands sometimes trembled. He looked at his hands, I looked at his face, seeing only an arid indifference. When I gripped his hands once to stop the shaking, he simply closed his eyes.

The job offer would come. And I would turn it down.

In his townhouse he eventually wanders down the stairs to sit in the room with the monochrome paintings. This means that my visit is over but sometimes I follow along and stand a while in the doorway, watching the man stare at something that is not in the room. He is remembering or imagining and I'm not sure if he is aware of my presence but I know that his mind is tunneling back to the dead lands where the bodies are banked and waiting.

- 2 -

I sat in a taxi with Emma and her son, Stak, all three bodies muscled into the rear seat, and the boy checked the driver's ID and immediately began to speak to the man in an unrecognizable language.

I conferred quietly with Emma, who said he was studying Pashto, privately, in his spare time. Afghani, she said, to enlighten me further.

I muttered something about Urdu, reflexively, in self-defense, because this was the only word that came to mind under the circumstances.

We were leaning into each other, she and I, and she exaggerated the terms of our complicity, speaking from the side of her mouth for comic effect and telling me that Stak walked in circles in his room enunciating phrases in Pashto in accordance with instructions from the device clipped to his belt.

He was seated directly behind the driver and spoke into the plexiglass shield, undeterred by traffic noise and street construction. He was fourteen, foreign born, a slant tower, six-four and growing, his voice rushed and dense. The driver did not seem surprised to find himself exchanging words and phrases in his native language with a white boy. This was New York. Every living breathing genotype entered his cab at some point, day or night. And if this was an inflated notion, that was New York as well.

Two people on the TV screen in front of us were speaking remotely about bridge and tunnel traffic.

Emma asked when I'd start the new job. Two weeks from today. Which group, which division, which part of town. I told her a few things that I'd already told myself.

"Suit and tie."

"Yes."

"Close shave, shined shoes."

"Yes."

"You look forward to this."

"Yes I do."

"Will this transform you?"

"It will remind me that this is the man I am."

"Down deep," she said.

"Whatever there is of deep."

The driver slipped into the bus lane, temporarily gaining position, advantage, dominance, and he gestured backwards to the boy as he spoke, three lights ahead all green—Pashto, Urdu, Afghani—and I told Emma that we were riding in a taxicab with a driver who enters the bus lane illegally and drives at madman speeds with one hand on the wheel while he half-looks over his shoulder and converses with a passenger in a far-flung language. What does this mean?

"Are you going to tell me that he drives this way only when he speaks this language?"

"It means this is just another day."

She looked into the options below the screen and put her finger to the inch-square site marked OFF. Nothing happened. We were back in mainstream traffic moving slowly down Broadway and I told Emma, out of nowhere, that I wanted to stop using my credit card. I wanted to pay cash, to live a life in which it is possible to pay cash, whatever the circumstances. To live a life, I said again, examining the phrase. Then I leaned toward the screen and hit the OFF site. Nothing happened. We listened to Stak speak to the driver within the limits of his Pashto, intensely. Emma looked hard at the images on the screen. I waited for her to hit the OFF site.

She and her former husband, a man whose name she did not speak, went to Ukraine and found the boy in a facility for abandoned children. He was five or six years old and they took the risk and made the arrangements and flew him home to Denver, which would eventually share time with New York when the parents divorced and Emma came east.

These are just the barest boundaries, of course, and she took her time rounding out the story for me, over weeks, and even as her voice went weary with regret, I became absorbed in another kind of home, in what was most immediate, the touch, the half words, the blue bedsheets, Emma's name like babytalk at two in the morning.

Horns were making sporadic noise and Stak was still talking to the driver through the closed panels. Talking, shouting, listening, pausing for the right word or phrase. I spoke to Emma about my money. Money comes to mind, I speak about it, the fading numbers, the small discrepancies that turn up on the withdrawal slips that are spat out by the automated teller machines. I go home and look at the check register and do the simple arithmetic and there's an aberration of one dollar and twelve cents.

"A bank mistake, not your mistake."

"Maybe it's not even a bank mistake but something in the structure itself. Beyond the computers and grids and digital algorithms and intelligence agencies. It's the root, the source, I'm almost serious, where things fit together or slip apart. Three dollars and sixty-seven cents."

Traffic was stopped dead and I nudged the window switch and listened to the blowing horns approach peak volume. We were trapped in our own obsessive clamor.

"I'm talking about minor matters that define us."

I shut the window and thought about what I might say next. Faint sounds of news and weather kept coming from the screen at Emma's kneecaps.

"Those blanked-out eternities at the airport. Getting there, waiting there, standing shoeless in long lines. Think about it. We take off our shoes and remove our metal objects and then enter a stall and raise our arms and get body-scanned and sprayed with radiation and reduced to nakedness on a screen somewhere and then how totally helpless we are all over again as we wait on the tarmac, belted in, our plane eighteenth in line, and it's all ordinary, it's routine, we make ourselves forget it. That's the thing."

She said, "What thing?"

"What thing. Everything. It's the things we forget about that tell us who we are."

"Is this a philosophical statement?"

"Traffic jams are a philosophical statement. I want to take your hand and wedge it in my crotch. That's a philosophical statement."

Stak backed away from the partition. He sat upright and motionless, looking into vague space.

We waited.

"The man. The driver. He's a former member of the Taliban."

He said this evenly, maintaining his aimless look. We thought about it, Emma and I, and eventually she said, "This is true?"

"He said it, I heard it. Taliban. Involved in skirmishes, clashes, all kinds of operations."

"What else did you talk about?"

"His family, my family."

She did not like this. The light tone we'd evolved yielded to a silence. I imagined a pub where we might go after dropping off the kid, mobbed bodies at the bar, couples at three or four tables, spirited talk, women laughing. Taliban. How is it that so many end up here, those who flee terror and those who render it, all driving taxis.

We were in a taxi because Stak rejected the subway. The barbarian heat and stench of the platform. The standing and waiting. The crowded cars, the voice recordings, the bodies touching. Was he the species that rejected all the things we were supposed to tolerate as a way of maintaining our shaky hold on common order?

We were quiet for a time and I hit the OFF site and then Emma hit it and I hit it again. The horns diminished but traffic did not move and the noise was soon resurgent, a few warped drivers prompting others and then others and the amplified sound becoming an independent force, noise for the sake of noise, overwhelming the details of time and place.

Traffic jam, downtown, Sunday, senseless.

Stak said, "If you close your eyes, the noise becomes a sound that's more or less normal. It doesn't go away, it just becomes something you hear because your eyes are closed. It becomes your sound."

"And when you open your eyes, what?" his mother said.

"The sound becomes noise again."

Why adopt a boy that age, five or six or seven, someone you see for the first time in a city you've never heard of, many miles from the capital, in a country that was itself an adoptee, passed from master to master through the centuries. She'd told me that her husband had Ukrainian roots but for her part I knew it had to be something in the boy's face, in his eyes, a need, a plea, and she felt a compassion that overwhelmed her. She saw a life bereft of expectation and it was hers to take and save, to make meaningful. But there was also, wasn't there, a kind of split-secondness, a gamble in the form of flesh-and-blood, let's just do it, and a brisk dismissal of all the things that could go wrong. And would this stranger in the house bring with him the long run of luck that might save their marriage?

She said that Stak counted pigeons on the rooftop across the street and never failed to report the number. Seventeen, twenty-three, a disappointing twelve.

Then, standing on the sidewalk, not a homeless man with sagging face and crayoned sign, begging, but a woman in meditative stance, body erect in long skirt and loose blouse, arms bent above her head, fingers not quite touching. Her eyes were closed and she was motionless, naturally so, with a small boy next to her. I'd seen the woman before, or different women, here and there, arms at sides or crossed at chest level, eyes always closed, and now the boy, first time, pressed trousers, white shirt, blue tie, looking a little scared, and until now I never wondered what the cause was or why there was no sign, no leaflets or tracts, only the woman, the stillness, the fixed point in the nonstop swarm. I watched her, knowing that I could not invent a single detail of the life that pulsed behind those eyes.

Traffic began to move and Stak was talking to the driver again, forehead welded to the plexiglass.

"Sometimes I tell him to shut up and eat his spinach. It took him a while," she said, "to understand that this is a joke."

He was here for a long weekend now and then and for ten days when the school year ended. This was all. She hadn't told me why she and her husband split up and there must be a reason why I never asked. To honor her reticence, perhaps, or was it more essentially that we were two individuals exploring a like-mindedness, determined to keep clear of the past, defy any impulse to recite our histories. We weren't married, we didn't live together but we were braided tight, each person part of the other. This is how I thought of it. An intuitive link, a reciprocal, one number related to another in such a way that when multiplied together, day or night, their product is one.

"He doesn't understand jokes and this is interesting because his father used to say the same thing about me."

Emma was a counselor in a year-round school for children with learning disabilities and developmental problems. Emma Breslow. I liked to say the name. I liked to tell myself that I would have guessed the name, or invented it, if she hadn't told me what it is at the wedding of mutual friends on a horse farm in Connecticut, where we first met. Would this become a nostalgic theme to return to in future years? Country roads, bluegrass pastures, bride and groom in riding boots. The idea of future years was too broad and open a topic for us to explore.

The towers grew taller here and the driver simply drove, letting Stak rehearse his Pashto. Two young women crossed at the light, heads shaved, and the man and woman on the screen spoke in faraway tones about a new surge of Arctic melt and we waited for footage of some kind, amateur video or network helicopter, but they changed the subject and I hit the OFF site and they were still there and then Emma hit it and I hit it again, calmly, and we resigned ourselves to the deadly sedative tenor of picture and sound.

Then she said, "He talks about the weather all the time. Not just today's weather but the general phenomenon narrowed down to certain places. Why is Phoenix always hotter than Tucson even though Tucson is farther south? He does not tell me the answer. This is not something I would know, it is something he would know, and he has no intention of sharing the knowledge. He likes to recite temperatures. The numbers tell him something. Tucson one hundred and three degrees fahrenheit. He always specifies fahrenheit or celsius. He relishes both words. Phoenix one hundred and seven degrees fahrenheit. Baghdad. What is Baghdad today?

"He's interested in climate."

"He's interested in numbers. High, medium, low. Place-names and numbers. Shanghai, he will say. Zero point zero one inches precipitation. Mumbai, he will say. He loves to say Mumbai. Mumbai. Yesterday, ninety-two degrees fahrenheit. Then he gives celsius. Then he checks one of his devices. Then he gives today. Then he gives tomorrow. Riyadh, he will say. He is disappointed when Riyadh loses out to another city. An emotional letdown."

"You're exaggerating."

"Baghdad, he will say. One hundred and thirteen degrees fahrenheit. Riyadh. One hundred and nine degrees fahrenheit. He is making me disappear. His size, his presence in a room, he shrinks our apartment, can't stay in one place, roams and talks, recites from memory, and his demands, his ultimatums, and the voice that issues them, with its own echo. I'm exaggerating slightly."

The cab was edging its way through the constricted streets downtown and if Stak heard what his mother was saying he gave no sign. He was speaking English now, trying to guide the driver in and out of the board game of one way and dead end.

"I don't know who he is, I don't know who his friends are, I don't know who his parents were."

"He didn't have parents. He had a biological mother and father."

"I hate the phrase *biological mother*. It's like science fiction. He reads science fiction, terminal amounts. That's something I know."

"And he leaves when?"

"Tomorrow."

"And you will feel what when he's gone?"

"I'll miss him. The minute he's out the door."

I gave this remark a chance to settle in the air.

"Then why don't you demand more time with him?"

"I couldn't bear it," she said. "And neither could he."

The taxi stopped on a near empty street just below the pit of finance and Stak angled his body out the door and jiggled a hand behind him in an ironic farewell. We watched him enter a loft building where he would spend the next two hours in a room choked with dust and stink, learning the principles of jujitsu, a method of artful self-defense predating the current practice of judo.

The driver slid open the middle panel and Emma paid him. We walked for a time, going nowhere, streets that had a feel of abandonment, fire hydrant open to a limp stream of rusty water.

After a while she said, "He invented the Taliban story."

Another idea for me to absorb.

"You know this?"

"He improvises now and then, inflates something, expands something, takes a story to a limit in a way that may or may not test your standards of belief. The Taliban was fiction."

"You sensed it right away."

"More than that. I knew it," she said.

"Fooled me."

"I'm not sure about his motive. I don't think there is a motive. It's a kind of recurring experiment. He's testing himself and me and you and everybody. Or it's pure instinct. Think of something, then say it. What he imagines becomes real. Not so strange really. Except I'd like to hit him with a frying pan sometimes."

"What about his jujitsu?"

"It's real, it's serious, I was allowed to watch one time. His body is willing to follow a strict format if he respects the tradition. The tradition is samurai combat. Feudal warriors."

"Fourteen years old."

"Fourteen."

"Never mind thirteen or fifteen. Fourteen is the final bursting forth," I said.

"Did you burst forth?"

"I'm still waiting to burst forth."

We fell into long silences, walking inward, step by step, and a light rain did not prompt a word or send us into cover. We walked north to the antiterror barricades on Broad Street where a tour leader spoke to his umbrella'd group about the scars on the wall caused by an anarchist's bomb a hundred years ago. We went along empty streets and our shared stride began to feel like a heartbeat and soon became a game, a tacit challenge, the pace quickening. The sun reappeared seconds before the rain stopped and we went past an untended shish kebab cart and saw a skateboarder sailing past at the end of the street, there and gone, and we approached a woman in Arab headdress, white woman, white blouse, stained blue skirt, talking to herself and walking back and forth, barefoot, five steps east, five steps west along a sidewalk webbed with scaffolding. Then the Money Museum, the Police Museum, the old stone buildings on Pine Street and our pace increased again, no cars or people here, just the iron posts, the stunted security markers set along the street, and I knew she'd outrace me, keep an even measure, she was will-driven just walking to a mailbox with a postcard in her hand. A sound around us that we could not identify made us stop and listen, the tone, the pitch, a continuous low dull hum, inaudible until you hear it and then it's everywhere, every step you take, coming from the empty buildings on both sides of the street, and we stood outside the locked revolving doors of Deutsche Bank listening to the systems within, the networks of interacting components. I grabbed her arm and moved her into the doorway of a shuttered storefront and we clutched and pressed and came close to outright screwing.

Then we looked at each other, still without a word, one of those looks that says who the hell are you anyway. This was her look. Women own this look. What am I doing here and who am I with, some fool who bubbles up out of nowhere. We were still in the early times and even if the romance endured it would continue to resemble the early times. We needed nothing further to discover and this is not the cold contractual reckoning it may seem. It is only who we were and how we talked and felt. We resumed our walk, casually now, seeing a barechested old man in rolled-up pajama bottoms sunbathing in a wet beach chair on a tenement fire escape. This was everything. We understood that the grain of our shared awareness, the print, the scheme, would remain stamped as in the first days and nights.

We wandered slowly back to the street where we'd started and I realized we were walking into a certain kind of mood, Emma's, a subdued disposition that took its shape from the imminent presence of her son. We reached the loft building and when he appeared he was carrying his gear in a knotted bundle, which he would take with him to Denver. We walked north and west and I found myself imagining that the man at the wheel of the taxi we hailed would have a Ukrainian name and accent and would be glad to speak the language with Stak, giving the boy another chance to turn a stranger's scant life into lavish fiction.

- 3 -

I keep checking the stove after turning off the burners. At night I make sure the door is locked and then go back to whatever I was doing but eventually sneak back to the door, inspect the lock, twist the door handle in order to verify, confirm, test the truth of, before going to bed. When did this begin? I walk down the street checking my wallet and then my keys. Wallet in left rear pocket, keys in right front pocket. I feel and pat the wallet from outside the pocket and sometimes stick my thumb in the pocket to touch the wallet itself. I don't do this for the keys. It's enough for me to make contact from outside the pocket, clutching the ring of keys within the doubled fabric of trouser pocket and handker-chief. I don't find it necessary to wrap the keys in the hand-kerchief. The keys are under the handkerchief. I tell myself that this arrangement is less unsanitary than the scenario of keys wrapped in handkerchief, if and when I blow my nose.

I visited Ross in his room of monochrome paintings, where he sat thinking and I sat waiting. He had asked me to come, saying there was an idea he wanted to propose. It occurred to me that this was his isolation cell, the formal site of every enshrined memory. He closed his eyes, let his head fall forward and then, as if in prescribed order, he watched his hand begin to tremble.

When it stopped he turned my way.

"Yesterday after I washed my face I looked in the mirror, seriously and deliberately looked. And I found myself becoming disoriented," he said, "because in a mirror left is right and right is left. But this wasn't the case. What was supposed to be my false right ear was my true right ear."

"That's how it seemed."

"That's how it was."

"There ought to be a discipline called the physics of illusions."

"There is but they call it something else."

"That was yesterday. What happened today?" I said.

He had no answer for this.

Then he said, "We had a cat for a time. I don't think you knew this. The cat would come down here and curl on the rug and there was a certain kind of stillness, a special grace, Artis said, that the cat brought to the room. The cat became inseparable from the paintings, the cat belonged to the art. When the cat was here we spoke softly and tried not to make an abrupt or unnecessary movement. It would betray the cat. I think we were serious about this. It would betray the cat, Artis said, and she had that smile she used when she was being a character in an old English movie. It would betray the cat."

His beard came spilling out of his face, freer and whiter

than the architectural models of the past. He spent much of his time in this room, growing old. I think he came here to grow old. He told me that he was in the process of donating some of his art to institutions and giving a few smaller pieces to friends. This is why he'd asked me to come here. He knew that I admired the art on these walls, paintings variously subdued, oil on canvas, all five. Then there was the sparely furnished room itself bearing a measure of such express intent that a person might feel his presence was a violation. I was not that sensitive.

We discussed the paintings. He had learned the language, I had not, but our way of seeing was not so different, it turned out. Light, balance, color, rigor. He wanted to give me a painting. Select one, it's yours, and possibly more than one, he said, and beyond that, there is the subject of where you want to live eventually.

I let this final remark linger. It surprised me, his belief that I might want to live here at some unspecified future time. He spoke of the possibility in a practical way, a matter of family business, but he was not thinking about the dollar value of the place. I heard a tentative note, a hint of innocent curiosity in his voice. He may have been asking me who I was.

He was leaning forward, I was sitting back.

I told him that I didn't know how to live here. This was a handsome brownstone with a front door of carved oak, a wood-paneled interior sedately furnished. My remark was not delivered purely for effect. I would be a tourist here, bound to a temporary arrangement. It was Artis who had brought him down from his penthouse duplex with lush decor, sun-drenched gardens and sweeping views of atomic sunsets. These were the things that suited his global ego in those earlier years. You have two majestic balconies, she'd told him, one more than the Pope. Here, some of his art, all of his books, whatever he'd managed to learn, love and acquire.

I knew how to live where I was living, in an old building on the upper west side with a small sad inner courtyard in perennial shadow, a once grand lobby, a laundry room that needed flood insurance—in an apartment of traditional fittings, high ceilings, quiet neighbors, say hello to familiar faces on the elevator, stand with Emma on the hot tarred surface of the roof, at the western ledge, watching a storm come whipping across the river in our direction.

This is what I told him. But wasn't it more complicated than that? There was a punishing cut to these remarks, a cheap rejection dredged from the past. All these levels, these spiral binds of involvement, so integral to the condition we shared.

I told him that I was touched and suggested that we both think further. But I wasn't touched and didn't expect to think further. I told him that the room was impressive, with or without the cat. What I didn't tell him was that there were several photographs of Madeline in my apartment. Schoolgirl, young woman, mother with adolescent son. And how could I ever display these pictures in the hostile setting of my father's townhouse.

Emma had studied dance for a time, years earlier, and there was something streamlined about her, face and body, the walk, the stride, even the trimmed sentences. There were occasions when I imagined that she subjected the most ordinary moments to a detailed plan. These were the idle speculations of a man whose plotless days and nights had begun to define the way the world was folding up around him.

But she kept me free of total disaffection. She was my lover. The idea alone consoled me, the word itself, *lover*, the beautiful musical note, the hovering letter *v*. How I slipped into dumb reverie, examining the word, seeing it as woman-shaped, feeling like a teenager anticipating the day when he might tell himself that he has a lover.

We went to her place, a modest apartment in a prewar building, east side, and she showed me Stak's room, which I'd only glimpsed on earlier visits. A pair of ski poles standing in a corner, a cot with an army blanket, an enormous wall map of the Soviet Union. I was drawn to the map, searching the expanse for place-names I knew and those many I'd never encountered. This was the boy's memory wall, Emma said, a great arc of historic conflict that stretched from Romania to Alaska. On every visit there would come a time when he simply stood and looked, matching his strong personal recollections of abandonment with the collective memory of old crimes, the famines engineered by Stalin that killed millions of Ukrainians.

He talks with his father about recent events, she said. Doesn't have much to say to me. Putin, Putin, Putin. This is what he says.

I stood at the map and began to recite place-names aloud. I didn't know why I was doing this. Arkhangelsk and Semipalatinsk and Sverdlovsk. Was this poetry or history or a childlike ramble across an unknown surface? I imagined Emma joining me in this recitation, stressing every syllable, both of us, her body pressed to mine, Kirensk and Svobodny, and then I imagined us in her bedroom, where we took off our shoes and lay on the bed, reciting face to face, cities, rivers, republics, each of us removing an item of clothing for each place named, my jacket for Gorki, her jeans for Kamchatka, moving slowly onward to Kharkov, Saratov, Omsk, Tomsk, and I started feeling stupid at this point but went on for a moment longer, reciting inwardly in streams of nonsense, names in the form of moans, the vast landmass shaping a mystery in which to shroud our loving night.

But we were in Stak's room, not the bedroom, and I'd stopped reciting and stopped imagining but wasn't ready to abandon the map. There was so much to see and feel and be ignorant of, so much to not know, and there was also Chelyabinsk, right here, where the meteor had struck, and the Convergence itself buried somewhere on the map in the old U.S.S.R., hemmed in by China, Iran, Afghanistan and so on. Is it possible that I'd been there, in the midst of such deep and searing narratives, and here it all is, decades of upheaval flattened into place-names.

This was Stak's map, not mine, and I realized that his mother was no longer standing next to me but had wandered out of the room and back into local time and place.

The city seems flattened, everything near street level, construction scaffolds, repairwork, sirens. I look at people's faces, make an instantaneous study, wordless, of the person inside the face, then remember to look up into the solid geometries of tall structures, the lines, angles, surfaces. I've become a student of crossing lights. I like to dash across the street with the red seconds on the crossing light down to 3 or 4. There is always an extra second-and-a-fraction between the time when the light turns red for pedestrians and the time when the other light turns green for traffic. This is my safety margin and I welcome the occasion, crossing a broad avenue in a determined stride, sometimes a civilized jog. It makes me feel true to the system, knowing that unnecessary risk is integral to the code of urban pathology.

It was a day for parents to visit the school where Emma taught and she invited me to come along. The children had disabilities ranging from speech disorders to emotional problems. They faced obstacles to everyday learning, how to gain basic kinds of awareness, how to comprehend, how to fix words in proper sequence, how to acquire experience, become alert, become informed, find out.

I stood against the wall in a room filled with boys and girls who sat at a long table with coloring books, games and toys. The parents milled about smiling and chatting and there was reason to smile. The kids were lively and engaged, writing stories and drawing animals, those who were able to do these things, and I looked and listened, trying to absorb a sense of the lives that were in the act of happening in this breezy tumult of small mingled voices and large hovering bodies.

Emma came over and stood next to me gesturing to a girl who sat crouched over a jigsaw puzzle, a girl who feared taking a single step, here to there, minute to minute, and needed every word of support and often an encouraging nudge. Some days are better than others, Emma said, and this was the sentence that would stay with me. All these disorders had their respective acronyms but she said she did not use them. There is the boy at the end of the table who can't produce the specific motor movements that would allow him to speak words that others might understand. Nothing is natural. Phonemes, syllables, muscle tone, action of tongue, lips, jaw, palate. The acronym is CAS, she said, but did not translate the term. It seemed to her a symptom of the condition itself.

Soon she was back among the children and her authority was clear, her self-assurance, even in its gentlest temper, talking, whispering, moving a piece on a gameboard or simply watching a child or speaking with a parent. The scene everywhere in the room was happy and active but I felt frozen to the wall. I tried to imagine the child, this one or that one, the one who could not recognize patterns and shapes or the one who could not sustain attention or follow the most basic spoken direction. Look at the boy with the picture book of ABCs and try to see him at the end of the day, on the school bus, talking to other kids or looking out the window and what does he see and how is it different from what the driver sees, or the other kids, and being met at the corner of this street and that avenue by his mother or father or older brother or sister or the family nurse or housekeeper. None of this led me into the life itself.

But why should it? How could it?

There were other children in other rooms and a few I'd seen earlier wandering the halls where a parent or teacher guided them back to one room or another. The grown-ups. Will some of these children be able to venture into adulthood, become grown-ups in outlook and attitude, able to buy a hat, cross a street. I looked at the girl who could not take a step without sensing some predetermined danger. She was not a metaphor. Light brown hair, sunlit now, a natural blush on her face, an intent look, tiny hands, six years old, I thought, Annie, I thought, or maybe Katie, and I decided to leave before she was done playing the game in front of her, parents' day over, children free to move to the next activity.

Play a game, make a list, draw a dog, tell a story, take a step. Some days are better than others.

- 4 -

It was time finally and I called Silverstone and turned down the job. He said he understood. I wanted to say, No you don't, not everything, not the part that makes me interesting.

I'd been following the promising leads all along and had no choice but to keep at it, wondering now and then if I'd become obsolete. In the street, on a bus, within the touch-screen storm, I could see myself moving autonomically into middle age, an involuntary man, guided by the actions of his nervous system.

I said something about the job to Emma. Wasn't what I wanted, didn't meet my needs. She said even less in return. This was not surprising. She took things as they came, not passively or uncaringly but in the spirit of an intervening space. Him and her, here to there. This did not apply to Stak. Her son was what we talked about in one of our roof-top intervals, cloudy day, our customary place at the western ledge, and we watched a barge being towed downriver, inch by inch, discontinuously, with a few tall structures fragmenting our view.

"This is what he does now. Online wagering sites. He bets

on plane crashes, real ones, various odds posted depending on the airline, the country, the time frame, other factors. He bets on drone strikes. Where, when, how many dead."

"He told you this?"

"Terrorist attacks. Visit the site, examine the conditions, enter a bet. Which country, which group, numbers of dead. Always the time frame. Has to happen within a certain number of days, weeks, months, other variables."

"He told you this?"

"His father told me this. His father ordered him to stop. Assassinations of public figures ranging from heads of state to insurgent leaders and other categories. Odds depend on the individual's rank and country. Other available wagers, quite a few of them. Apparently a thriving site."

"I don't know how thriving. These things don't happen often."

"They happen. The people who place the bets expect them to happen, wait for them to happen."

"The bet makes the event more likely. I understand that. Ordinary people sitting at home."

"A force that changes history," she said.

"That's my line," I said.

Were we beginning to enjoy this? I glanced toward the other end of the roof to see a woman in sandals, shorts and a halter-top dragging a blanket to a spot where she seemed to expect the sun to touch down. I looked into the heavy cloud cover, then back to the woman.

"Do you talk to his father often?"

"We talk when necessary. The boy makes it necessary now and then. There are other habits, things he does."

"Talking to cabdrivers."

"Not worth a phone call to Denver."

"What else?"

"Altering his voice for days at a time. He has a sort of hollow voice he affects. I can't imitate it. A submerged voice, digital noise, sound units fitted together. Then there's the Pashto. He speaks Pashto to people in the street who look as though they might be native speakers. They nearly never are. Or to a supermarket clerk or a cabin attendant on a flight. The cabin attendant thinks this is the first stage in a hijacking. I witnessed this once, his father twice."

I found myself disturbed by the fact that she talked to his father. Of course they talked, they had to talk for any number of reasons. I imagined a sturdy man with darkish complexion, he is standing in a room with photos on the wall, father and son in hunting gear. He and the boy watch TV news on an obscure cable channel, programming from eastern Europe. I needed a name for Stak's father, Emma's ex, in Denver, mile-high.

"Has he stopped making bets on car bombs?"

"His father is not completely convinced. He makes surreptitious raids on Stak's devices."

The woman on the blanket was motionless, supremely supine, legs spread, arms spread, palms up, face up, eyes shut. Maybe she had news that the sun was due to appear, maybe she didn't want the sun, maybe she did this every day at the same time, a yielding, a discipline, a religion.

"He'll be returning in a couple of weeks. He has to appear at his jujitsu academy. His dojo," she said. "Special event."

Or maybe she just wanted to get out of the apartment, a

resident of the building but unknown to me, middle-aged, escaping the cubical life for a few hours, same as us, same as the hundreds we would see when we walked across the park to Emma's place, the runners, idlers, softball players, the parents pushing strollers, the palpable relief of being in unmetered space for a time, a scattered crowd safe in our very scatter, people free to look at each other, to notice, admire, envy, wonder at.

Think about it, I nearly said. So many places elsewhere, crowds collecting, thousands shouting, chanting, bending to the charge of police with batons and riot shields. My mind working into things, helplessly, people dead and dying, hands bound behind them, heads split open.

We began to walk faster because she wanted to get home in time to watch a tennis match at Wimbledon, her favorite player, the Latvian woman who groaned erotically with each fierce return.

If I'd never known Emma, what would I see when I walk the streets going nowhere special, to the post office or the bank. I'd see what is there, wouldn't I, or what I was able to assemble from what is there. But it's different now. I see streets and people with Emma in the streets and among the people. She's not an apparition but only a feeling, a sensation. I'm not seeing what I think she would be seeing. This is my perception but she is present within it or spread throughout it. I sense her, feel her, I know that she occupies something within me that allows these moments to happen, off and on, streets and people.

• • •

The twenty-dollar bills emerged from the slot in the automated teller machine and I stood in the booth counting the
money and turning some bills upside down and others back
to front to regularize the stack. I maintained reasonably, to
myself, that this procedure should have been performed by
the bank. The bank should deliver the money, my money, in
an orderly format, ten bills, twenty dollars each bill, all bills
face forward, face up, unsmudged money, sanitary money. I
counted again, head down, shoulders hunched, partitioned
from people in the booths to either side of me, isolated but
aware, feeling their presence left and right, my money held
near my chest. It didn't seem to be me. It seemed to be
someone else, a recluse who'd wandered into semi-public
view, standing here and counting.

I touched the screen for the receipt and then for account
activity and account summary and I wrapped the bills inside
the flimsy slips of toxic paper and left the booth, the stall,
receipts and money clutched in my hand. I didn't look at
the people in line. No one ever looks at anyone in the ATM
area. And I tried not to think about the security cameras
but here I was in my mind's self-surveillance device, body
crabbed tight as I removed the money from the slot, counted
it, organized it and then recounted it.

But was this really so introspective, so abnormally cautious? The handling of the bills, the heightened awareness,
isn't this something people do, check the wallet, check the
keys, it's just another level of the commonplace.

I sit at home with transaction registers, withdrawal slips,

records of account details, my outdated smartphone, my credit card statement, new balance, late payment, additional charges all spread before me on Madeline's old walnut desk and I try to determine the source of what appear to be several small persistent errors, deviations from the logic of the number concept, the pure thrust of reliable numbers that determine one's worth, even as totals diminish week by week.

I described the details of several job interviews to Emma, who enjoyed my accounts of the proceedings—voice imitations, sometimes verbatim, of interviewers' remarks. She understood that I was not ridiculing these men and women. This was a documentary approach to a special kind of dialogue and we both knew that the performer himself, still jobless, was the subject of the piece.

The sun was shining now and I thought of the woman spread-eagled on my roof. There are women everywhere, Emma in a director's chair a handclasp away from me and the Latvian woman and her opponent on the TV screen, sweating, groaning, swatting a tennis ball in patterns that might be subject to advanced study by behavioral scientists.

We hadn't had a serious discussion for an hour or so. I deferred to Emma at such times. She had an adopted son, a failed marriage, a job involving damaged children and I had what—access to a breezy rooftop with an interrupted view of the river.

She said, "I think you look forward to the job interviews. Shave the face, shine the shoes."

"I'm down to one decent pair of shoes. This is not rank neglect but a kind of day-to-day carelessness."

"Do you feel a certain affection for these decent shoes?"

"Shoes are like people. They adjust to situations."

We watched tennis and drank beer in tall glasses that she kept on their sides in the freezer compartment of her squat refrigerator. Frosted glasses, dark lager, point, game, match, one woman flipping her racket in the air, the other woman walking out of the frame, the first woman falling backwards to the grass court in glad abandon, arms stretched wide like the woman on my roof, whoever she was.

"Define a tennis racket. This is something I might have said to myself when I was in my early teens."

"Then you would do it," she said.

"Or try to."

"Tennis racket."

"Early teens."

I told her that I used to stand in a dark room, eyes shut, mind immersed in the situation. I told her that I still do it, although rarely, and that I never know that I'm about to do it. Just stand in the dark. The lamp sits on the bureau next to the bed. There I am, eyes shut. Sort of Staklike.

She said, "It sounds like a kind of formal meditation."

"I don't know."

"Maybe you're trying to empty the mind."

"You haven't done it yourself."

"Who, me, no."

"I'm shutting my eyes against the dark."

"And you're wondering who you are."

"Maybe in a blank way, if that's possible."

"What's the difference between eyes closed in a lighted room and eyes closed in a dark room?"

"All the difference in the world."

"I'm trying not to say something funny."

She said this in an even tone, with a serious face.

Know the moment, feel the gliding hand, gather all the forgettable fragments, fresh towels on the racks, nice new bar of soap, clean sheets on the bed, her bed, our blue sheets. This was all I needed to take me day to day and I tried to think of these days and nights as the hushed countermand, ours, to the widespread belief that the future, everybody's, will be worse than the past.

One of my father's people called with the details. Time, place, manner of dress. This was lunch — but why. I didn't need lunch in a midtown temple of cuisine art where jackets are required and the food and flower arrangements are said to be exquisite and the staff more competent than pallbearers at a state funeral. It was the weekend and my dress shirts were at the laundry being readied for the next wave of interviews. I had to wear a used and reused shirt, first spitting on my finger to wash the inside of the collar.

I'm always the first to arrive, I always get there first. I chose to wait at the table and when Ross showed up I was struck by the sight of him. The vested gray suit and bright tie set off his wildman beard and halting stride and I wasn't sure whether he resembled an impressive ruin or a famous stage actor currently living the role that defines his long career.

He slid inchingly into our velvet banquette.

"You didn't want the job. Turned it down."

"It wasn't right. I'm talking to an important person in an investment strategy group. It's a definite possibility."

"People out of work. You were offered a job in a strong company."

"Set of companies. But I was not dismissive. I considered every aspect."

"Nobody cares that you're my son. There are sons and daughters everywhere, in solid positions, doing productive work."

"Okay."

"You make too much of it. Father and son. You would have become your own man in a matter of days."

"Okay."

"People out of work," he said again, reasonably.

We talked and ordered and I kept looking into his face, thinking of a certain word. I think of words that lead me into dense realities, clarifying a situation or a circumstance, at least in theory. Here was Ross, eyes tired and shoulders hunched, right hand trembling slightly, and the word was *desuetude*. The word had a stylish quality suited to the environment. But what did it mean? A state of inaction, I thought, maybe a lost energy. I was looking at Ross Lockhart, handsomely outfitted but minus the relentlessness and craft that had shaped the man.

"Last time I was here about five years ago I talked Artis into coming along. Her health was not yet approaching drastic decline. I don't recall all that much. But there was one point, one interval. It's very clear. One particular moment. She looked at a woman being led past us to a nearby table.

She waited for the woman to be seated and looked a while longer. Then she said, 'If she were wearing any more makeup she would burst into flames.'"

I laughed at that and noted how the memory remained alive in his eyes. He was seeing Artis across the table, across the years, a kind of waveform, barely discernible. The wine arrived and he managed to look at the label and then to perform the ceremonial swirl and taste but he hadn't sniffed the cork and did not indicate approval of the wine. He was still remembering. The waiter took a while to decide that it was permissible to pour. I watched all this, innocently, as an adolescent might.

I said, "They're called Selected Assets Inc."

"Who's that?"

"The people I'm talking to."

"Buy yourself another shirt. That may help them make up their mind," he said.

When does a man become his father? I was nowhere near the time but it occurred to me that it could happen one day while I sat staring at a wall, all my defenses assimilated into the matching moment.

Food arrived and he began to eat at once while I looked and thought. Then I told him a story that made him pause.

I told him how his wife, the first, my mother, had died, at home, in her bed, unable to talk or listen or to see me sitting there. I'd never told him this and I didn't know why I was telling him now, the hours I'd spent at her bedside, Madeline, with the neighbor in the doorway leaning on her cane. I found myself going into some detail, recalling whatever I could, speaking softly, describing the scene. The neighbor, the cane, the bed, the bedspread. I described the bedspread. I mentioned the old oak bureau with carved wings for handles. He would remember that. I think I wanted him to be touched. I wanted him to see the last hours as they happened. There was no dark motive. I wanted us to be joined in this. And how curious it was to be speaking about it here, amid the tiptoe waiters and the stalks of white amaryllis set along the walls, funereally, and the single white orchid in the small vase at the center of our table. There was no bitter theme running through these remarks. The scene itself, in Madeline's room, would not permit it. The table, the lamp, the bed, the woman in the bed, the cane with the splayed legs.

We sat thinking and after a time one of us took a bite of food and a sip of wine and then the other did too. Everywhere in the room a vibrant tide of conversation, something I hadn't noticed until now.

"Where was I when this happened?"

"You were on the cover of *Newsweek*."

I watched him try to make sense of this and then explained that I'd seen the magazine with my father on the cover just before learning that my mother was in critical condition.

He leaned farther down toward the table, the back of his hand propping his chin.

"Do you know why we're here?"

"You said you were last here with Artis."

"And she is forever part of what we are here to discuss."

"It seems too soon."

"It's all I think about," he said.

All he thinks about. Artis in the chamber. I think about her also, now and then, shaved and naked, standing and waiting. Does she know she's waiting? ls she wait-listed? Or is she simply dead and gone, beyond the smallest tremor of self-awareness?

"It's time to be going back," he said. "And I want you to come with me."

"You want a witness."

"I want a companion."

"I understand."

"One person only. No one else," he said. "I'm in the process of making arrangements."

He would empty out his years on the long plane journey. I imagined him losing all his Lockhartness, becoming Nicholas Satterswaite. How a tired life collapses into its origins. Thousands of air miles, all those amorphous hours of day-night numbness. Are we the Satterswaites, he and I? *Desuetude.* It occurred to me that the word might be applied more surely to the son than to the father. Disuse, misuse. Wasted time as a life pursuit.

"You still believe in the idea."

"Heart and mind," he said.

"But isn't it an idea that no longer carries the inner conviction it used to have?"

"The idea continues to gain strength in the only place that matters."

"Back to the numbered levels," I said.

"We've been through all this."

"A long time ago. Doesn't it feel that way? Two years. Feels like half a lifetime."

"I'm making arrangements."

"You just said that. The ass-end of civilization. We'll go, why not, you and I. Make the arrangements."

I waited for what was coming next.

"And you'll think about the other matters."

"I don't want a painting. I don't want what people are supposed to want. It's not that I've renounced material things. I'm not an ascetic. I live comfortably enough. But I want to keep it small."

He said, "I need to leave clear instructions."

"I don't chase after money. I think of money as something to count. It's something I put in my wallet and take out of my wallet. Money is numbers. You say that you need to leave clear instructions. Clear instructions sound intimidating. I like to drift into things."

Plates and cutlery were gone and we were drinking an aged Madeira. Maybe all Madeiras are aged. The restaurant was emptying out and I liked watching them, all these people striding decisively back to their situations, their endeavors. They had to return to office suites and conference rooms and I did not. It gave me a free sense of being outside the established course of executive routine when in fact what I was out of was a job.

We did not speak, Ross and I. The waiter was at the far end of the room, a still figure framed by bunched flowers in hanging baskets, and he was waiting to be summoned for the check. I wanted to believe it was raining so we could walk out the door into the rain. In the meantime we thought about the journey ahead and we drank our fortified wine.

- 5 -

I watch Emma stand before the full-length mirror. She is seeing that everything is in place before she leaves for school, for the eager or somber or intractable children. Shirt and vest, tailored slacks, casual shoes. On an impulse I walk into the image and stand next to her. We look for a number of seconds, the pair of us, without comment or self-consciousness or any sign of amusement, and I understand that this is a telling moment.

Here we are, the woman smart, determined, not detached so much as measuring every occasion, including this one, brown hair swept back, a face that is not interested in being pretty, and this gives her a quality I can't quite name, a kind of undividedness. We are seeing each other as never before, two sets of eyes, the meandering man, taller, bushy-haired, narrow face, slightly recessed chin, faded jeans and so on.

He is a man on line for tickets to a ballet that a woman wants to see and he is willing to wait for hours while she tends her schoolchildren. She is the woman, rigid in her seat, watching a dancer splice the air, fingertips to toes.

Here we are, all this and more, things that normally

escape the inquiring eye, a single searching look, so much to see, each of us looking at both of us, and then we shake it all off and walk down four flights into the pitch of street noise that tells us we're back among the others, in unsparing space.

Nearly a week went by before we spoke again, on the telephone.

"Day after tomorrow."

"If you want me to come by."

"I'll mention it to him. We'll see. Things have tightened up," she said.

"What happened?"

"He doesn't want to go back to school. They resume in August. He's saying it's a waste of time. It's all dead time. There's nothing they can say that means anything to him."

I stood by the window holding the phone and looking down at my shoes, which I'd just shined.

"Does he have some kind of alternative?"

"I've asked that question repeatedly. The boy is noncommittal. His father sounds helpless."

I was not unhappy to hear that his father was helpless. Then, again, I felt awful knowing that Emma was apparently in the same state.

"Offhand I don't know how I can help. But I'll think about it. I'll think about myself at that age. And if he's agreeable maybe we'll repeat the cab ride to the dojo."

"He doesn't want to go to the dojo. He's done with jujitsu. He agreed to this visit only because I insisted."

I pictured her grimly insisting, standing straight, speaking rapidly, cellphone gripped tight. She said she'd talk to him and give me a call.

It was unnerving to hear this, that she'd give me a call. This is what I heard at the end of job interviews. There was an appointment coming up in less than an hour and I'd shined my shoes with the traditional polish, the horsehair brush and the flannel cloth, rejecting an instant shine with the all-color sponge. Then I looked at my face in the bathroom mirror, double-checking the effectiveness of the close shave I'd given myself twenty minutes earlier. I recalled something Ross had said about his right ear in the mirror being his real right ear instead of the mirror-image left ear. I had to concentrate hard to convince myself that this was not the case.

Things people do, ordinarily, forgettably, things that breathe just under the surface of what we acknowledge having in common. I want these gestures, these moments to have meaning, check the wallet, check the keys, something that draws us together, implicitly, lock and relock the front door, inspect the burners on the stove for dwindling blue flame or seeping gas.

These are the soporifics of normalcy, my days in middling drift.

I saw her again one morning, the woman in the stylized pose, this time alone, no small boy at her side. She stood on a corner near Lincoln Center and I was certain it was the same woman, eyes closed as before, arms this time down near her sides but held away from her body in a stance of sudden alarm. She was frozen in place. But maybe that's wrong. She had simply pledged herself into a mental depth, facing in toward the sidewalk and the people hurrying past. A teenage girl stopped just long enough to aim her device and take a picture. A disturbance building all around us, air thick and dark, sky ready to crack open, and I wondered if she would remain in place when the rain hit.

Again I noted that there was no indication of her cause, her mission. She stood in open space, an unexplained presence. I wanted to see a small table with leaflets or a poster in a foreign language. I wanted a language in a non-Roman alphabet. Give me something to go on. There was a quality, a tone, the cast of her features that suggested she was from another culture. I wanted a sign in Mandarin, Greek, Arabic, Cyrillic, a plea from a woman who belongs to a group or a faction that is somehow threatened by forces here or abroad.

Foreign, yes, but I assumed she spoke English. I told myself that I could see it in her face, a kind of transnational bearing, an adaptation.

If this were a man, I thought, would I stop and watch?

I had to keep watching. Others glanced, two kids took pictures, a man wearing an apron hurried past, street pace quickened by the threat of weather.

I approached, careful not to get too close.

I said, "I wonder if I might ask a question."

No response, face the same, arms stiff, regimental.

I said, "Up to now, I haven't tried to guess what your purpose is, your cause. And if there was a poster, I can't help thinking it might convey a message of protest."

I took a step back, for effect, although she could not see me. I don't think I expected a response. The idea that she might open her eyes and look at me. The possibility of a few words. Then I realized that I'd started by saying I would ask a question and I hadn't done this.

I said, "And the boy in the white shirt and blue tie. Last time, downtown somewhere, there was a boy with you. Where is the boy?"

We remained in place. People maneuvering for position, traditional taxi panic, and it wasn't even raining yet. A sign in Mandarin, Cantonese, a few words in Hindi. I needed a specific challenge to help me counteract the random nature of the encounter. A woman. Did it have to be a woman? Would anyone pause to look if a man stood here in an identical posture? I tried to imagine a man with a sign in Phoenician, circa one thousand B.C. Why was I doing this to myself? Because the mind keeps working, uncontrollably. I moved closer again and faced her directly, mainly to discourage those who wanted to take her picture. The man wearing an apron came back this way, pushing a series of interlocked shopping carts, four carts, empty. The woman with eyes ever closed, she fixed things in place, stopped traffic for me, allowed me to see clearly what was here.

Had I made a mistake, talking to her? It was intrusive and stupid. I'd betrayed something in my register of cautious behavior and I'd violated the woman's will toward a decisive silence.

I stood there for twenty minutes, waiting to see how she

would react to the rain. I wanted to stay longer, would have stayed longer, felt guilty about leaving, but the rain did not come and I had to set out for my next appointment.

Didn't Artis tell me once that she spoke Mandarin?

We found a nearly empty restaurant not far from the gallery. Stak ordered broccoli, nothing with it. Good for the bones, he said. He had a long face and stand-up hair and wore a jogging suit that zippered up the back.

Emma told him to finish the story he'd started telling us in the taxi.

"Okay so I began to wonder where Oaxaca is. I guessed it's in Uruguay or Paraguay, mainly Paraguay, even though I was ninety percent sure it's in Mexico because of the Toltecs and the Aztecs."

"What's the point?"

"I used to need to know things at once. Now I think about them. Oaxaca. What do you have? You have *o a* and then *x a* and then *c a*. Wa há ca. I denied myself knowledge about the population of Oaxaca or the ethnic breakdown or even for sure what language they speak, which could be Spanish or some Indian language mixed with Spanish. And I situated the place somewhere where it doesn't belong."

I'd told Emma about the art gallery and the lone object on display and she told Stak and he agreed to take a look. An accomplishment in itself.

It was clear that I was the go-between, recruited to ease the tension between them, and I found myself headed directly into the sensitive subject itself.

"You're done with school."

"We're done with each other. We don't need each other. Day to day is one more wasted day."

"Maybe I know the feeling, or remember it. Teachers, subjects, fellow students."

"Meaningless."

"Meaningless," I said. "But other kinds of school, less formal, with independent research, time to explore a subject thoroughly. I know you've been through all this."

"I've been through all this. It's all a bunch of faces. I ignore faces."

"How do you do that?"

"We learn to see the differences among the ten million faces that pass through our visual field every year. Right? I unlearned this a long time ago, in childhood, in my orphanage, in self-defense. Let the faces pass through the vision box and out the back of your head. See them all like one big blurry thing."

"With a few exceptions."

"Very few," he said.

There was nothing he cared to add.

I looked at him intently and said in the most deliberate voice I could manage, "'Rocks are, but they do not exist.'"

After a pause I said, "I came across this statement when I was in college and forgot it until very recently. 'Man alone exists. Rocks are, but they do not exist. Trees are, but they do not exist. Horses are, but they do not exist.'"

He was listening, head bent, eyes narrowed. His shoulders squirmed a little, fitting themselves to the idea. *Rocks are.* We were here to see a rock. The object on exhibit was officially designated an interior rock sculpture. It was a large rock, one rock. I told Stak that this is what raised the statement from the far corners of my undergraduate mind.

"'God is, but he does not exist.'"

What I did not tell him was that these ideas belong to Martin Heidegger. I hadn't known until fairly recently that this was a philosopher who'd maintained a firm fellowship with Nazi principles and ideologies. History everywhere, in black notebooks, and even the most innocent words, *tree*, *horse*, *rock*, gone dark in the process. Stak had his own twisted history to think about, mass starvation of his forebears. Let him imagine an uncorrupted rock.

The show had been installed a couple of decades earlier, still running, ever running, same rock, and I'd visited three times in recent years, always the lone witness except for the attendant, the guardian, a late-middle-aged woman seated at the far end of the gallery wearing a black Navajo hat with a feather in the band.

Stak said, "I used to throw rocks at fences. There was nowhere else to throw a rock except at people and I had to stop doing people or they'd put me in detention and feed me fertilizer twice a day."

A buoyancy in his voice, the self-approbation of a fourteen-year-old, and who could blame him. We were getting along pretty well, he and I. Maybe it was the broccoli. His mother sat next to him, saying nothing, looking at nothing, listening to us, yes, warily, not knowing what it was that the boy might say next.

I insisted on paying for lunch and Emma yielded, accepting my role as troop leader. The gallery occupied the entire third floor of an old loft building. We trekked up the stairs single-file and there was something about the cramped passage, the weak lighting, the stairs themselves and the walls themselves that made me think we'd been transformed into black-and-white, drained of skin pigment and the color values of our clothing.

The room was long and wide with plank floorboards and chipped and dented walls. The old bicycle belonging to the attendant was propped against the far wall next to her folding chair, no sign of the woman herself. But here was the rock itself, braced on a solid metal slab about three inches high. There were strips of white tape on the floor that marked visitor limits. Get close but don't touch. Emma and I paused, half a room away, setting the rock in noble perspective. Stak wasted no time, striding directly to the object, which was taller than he was, and finding everything he needed to look at, all the irregularities of surface, the projections and indentations that belong to a rock, a boulder in this case, general shape somewhat rounded, maybe six feet across at its broadest point.

We approached slowly, she and I, quietly, but was it out of churchlike respect for the rock sculpture, the natural artwork, or were we simply observing the joined form of object and observer—the elusive boy who rarely attaches himself to something solid. Of course he reached across the taped border and managed to touch the rock, barely, and I felt his mother heed an inner pause, a caution, waiting for an alarm to start wailing. But the rock simply sat there.

We stood to either side of him and I allowed myself a minute or two with the rock.

Then I said, "Okay, go ahead."

"What?"

"Define *rock*."

I was thinking of myself at his age, determined to find the more or less precise meaning of a word, to draw other words out of the designated word in order to locate the core. This was always a struggle and the current instance was no different, a chunk of material that belongs to nature, shaped by forces such as erosion, flowing water, blowing sand, falling rain.

The definition needed to be concise, authoritative.

Stak yawned outstandingly, then leaned away from the rock, appraising it, measuring the thing from a certain distance, its physical parameters, solid surface, its crags, snags, spurs and pits, and he walked around it, noting the whole unhoned expanse.

"It's hard, it's rock hard, it's petrified, it has major mineral content or it's all mineral with the long-dead remains of plants and animals fossilized inside it."

He spoke some more, arms drawn to his chest, hands mixing the fragments of his remarks, phrase by phrase. He was alone with the rock, a thing requiring a single syllable to give it outline and form.

"Officially let's say a rock is a large hard mass of mineral substance lying on the ground or embedded in the soil."

I was impressed. We kept looking at it, three of us, with traffic blasting by outside.

Stak talked to the rock. He told it that we were looking at it. He referred to us as three members of the species *H. sapiens*. He said that the rock would outlive us all, probably outlive the species itself. He went on for a while and then addressed no one in particular, saying there are three kinds of rock. He named them before I could attempt to recall the names and he spoke about petrology and geology and marble and calcite, and his mother and I listened while the boy grew taller. The attendant walked in then. I preferred to think of her as the curator, same woman, same feathered hat, a T-shirt and sandals, baggy denims fitted with bicycle clips. She carried a small paper bag, said nothing, went to her chair and took a sandwich out of the bag.

We watched her openly, in silence. The huge gallery area, nearly bare, and the one prominent object on display lent a significance to the simplest movement, man or woman, dog or cat. After a pause I asked Stak about another kind of nature, the weather, and he said he was no longer involved with the weather. He said the weather was long gone. He said that some things become de-necessitated.

His mother spoke then, at last, in a tense whisper.

"Of course you're involved. The temperature, celsius and fahrenheit, and the cities, one hundred and four degrees, one hundred and eight degrees. India, China, Saudi Arabia. What happened to make you say you're not involved? Of course you're involved. Where did it all go?"

Her voice sounded lost and on this day everything about her suggested a lost time. Her son about to return to his father and then what happens, where's the future if he doesn't go back to school, what lies waiting? A son or daughter who travels at a wayward angle must seem a penalty the parent must bear — but for what crime?

I reminded myself that I needed a name for Stak's father.

Before we left, the boy called across the room to the curator, asking her how they got the rock into the building. She was in the process of lifting the curved end of one slice of her bread in order to inspect the interior of the sandwich. She said they made a hole in the wall and hoisted the thing from a flatbed truck equipped with a crane. I'd thought of asking the same question the first time I was here but decided it was interesting to imagine the thing always here, undocumented.

Rocks are, but they do not exist.

On our way down the dim stairway I quoted the remark again and Stak and I tried to figure out what it means. It was a subject that blended well with our black-and-white descent.

I listen to classical music on the radio. I read the kind of challenging novel, often European, sometimes with a nameless narrator, always in translation, that I tried to read when I was an adolescent. Music and books, simply there, the walls, the floor, the furniture, the slight misalignment of two pictures that hang on the living room wall. I leave objects as they are. I look and let them be. I study every physical minute.

Two days later she showed up unannounced, never happened before, and she'd never been so clumsy and rushed, not slipping out of her jeans but fighting her way out, needing to rid herself of the seething sort of tensions that accompany any matter involving her son.

"He embraced me and left. I don't know what scared me more, the leave-taking or the embrace. This is the first time totally that he volunteered an embrace."

It appeared that she was undressing just to undress. I stood at the foot of the bed, shirt on, pants on, shoes and socks, and she kept undressing and kept talking.

"Who is this kid? Did I ever see him before? Here he is, there he goes. Embraced me and left. Goes where? He's not my son, never was."

"He was, he is. Every inch the boy you took out of the orphanage. Those missing years. His years," I said. "You knew the moment you first saw him that he carried something you could never claim as your rightful due, except legally."

"Orphanage. Sounds like a word out of the sixteenth century. The orphan boy becomes a prince."

"A prince regent."

"A princeling," she said.

I laughed, she did not. All the command she'd demonstrated with the children in the schoolroom, there and elsewhere, the woman in the mirror knowing who she is and what she wants, all undermined by the boy's brief visit, and here was the urgency of her need to break free, a flail of limbs on my messy bed.

I would see her less often after this, call and wait for a return call, longer hours at her job, and she was quieter now, early dinner and then home, alone, rarely a word about her son except to say that he had given up his Pashto, stopped learning, stopped speaking except when there was a practical matter that needed to be addressed. Her remarks were delivered in an evenness of tone, from a sheltered distance.

I decided to go running. I wore a sweatshirt, jeans and sneakers and went running in the park, around the reservoir, rain or shine. There is a smartphone that has an app that counts the steps a person takes. I did my own count, day by day, stride for stride, into the tens of thousands.

- 6 -

The woman swiveled away from her desktop screen and looked at me for the first time. She was a recruiter and the job in question was listed as compliance and ethics officer for a college in western Connecticut. I repeated the term to myself periodically as we spoke, omitting western Connecticut, which was a three-dimensional entity. Hills, trees, lakes, people.

She said I'd be responsible for interpreting the school charter to determine regulatory requirements in the context of state and federal laws. I said fine. She said something about supervision, coordination and oversight. I said okay. She waited for questions but I didn't have a question. She threw in the term *bilateral mandate* and I told her that she resembled an actress whose name I didn't know, someone appearing in a recent revival of a play I hadn't seen. But I'd read about it, I said, and I'd looked at the photographs. The recruiter smiled faintly, her face becoming real in the amplified company of the actress. She understood that my remark was not an attempt to ingratiate myself. I was simply being self-distracted.

We spoke in a friendly way about theater and it was clear from this point on that she wanted to dissuade me from considering the position, not because I was underqualified or overeager but because I didn't belong there, in that environment. Compliance and ethics officer. She didn't realize that everything she'd reported about the position, in the authorized terminology of job listings, was suited to my preferences and central to my past experience.

People here and there, hands out, standing man with paper cup, woman crouched above her vomit in seasick colors, woman seated on blanket, body rocking, voice chanting, and I see this all the time and always pause to give them something and what I feel is that I don't know how to imagine the lives behind the momentary contact, the dollar contact, and what I tell myself is that I am obliged to look at them.

Taxis, trucks and buses. The noise persists even when traffic is stopped. I hear this from my rooftop, heat beating into my head. This is the noise that hangs in the air, nonstop, whatever time of day or night, if you know how to listen.

I didn't use my credit card for eight straight days. What's the point, what's the message. Cash leaves no trace, whatever that means.

The phone rings, recorded message from a state agency concerning massive disruptions of service. The voice does not say massive but this is how I interpret the message.

I check the stove after turning off the burners and then make sure the door is locked by unlocking it and then relocking it.

I look out the window at the streetlights and wait for someone to walk by, casting a long shadow in an old movie.

I feel a challenge to be equal to whatever is forthcoming. There is Ross and his need to confront the future. There is Emma and the tender revisions of our love.

The phone rings again, the same recorded message. I spend about two seconds wondering what kind of services will be disrupted. Then I try to think about all the phones of every type bearing this message, people in the millions, but no one will remember to mention it to anyone else because what we all know is not worth sharing.

Breslow was Emma's surname, not her husband's. I knew this much and I'd more or less settled on a first name for the man. Volodymyr. He was born in this country but I decided what's the point of giving him a name if it's not Ukrainian. Then I realized how wasteful this was, thinking this way, at this time, wasteful, shallow, callous, inappropriate.

Invented names belong to the strafed landscape of the desert, except for my father's and mine.

I wandered through the townhouse until I found him, at the kitchen table, eating a grilled cheese sandwich. Someone nearby was running a vacuum cleaner. He raised a hand in greeting and I asked how he was doing.

"I no longer take my classic morning crap after breakfast. Everything's slower and dumber."

"Should I be packing?"

"Pack light. I'm packing light," he said.

He was not trying to be funny.

"Is there a date? I'm interested to know because there's a job offer pending."

"Want something to eat? What kind of offer?"

"Compliance and ethics officer. Four days a week."

"Say it again."

"I'll have long weekends free," I said.

Ross had become a blue-denim'd man. He wore the pants every day, same pair, a casual blue shirt, gray running shoes without socks. I had a sandwich and a beer and the vacuuming gradually diminished and I tried to imagine the man's days and nights without the woman. All his privileges and comforts, drained of meaning now. Money. Has it been money, my father's money, that determines the way I think and live? Whether I accept what he offers or turn him down cold, is this what overwhelms everything else?

"When will I know?"

"Matter of days. You'll be contacted," he said.

"How?"

"However they do these things. I'm simply going away. I haven't been active professionally for some time and I'm simply going away."

"But there are people who know the purpose of the journey. Trusted associates."

"They know certain things. They know I have a son," he said. "And they know that I'm going away."

We went back to saying nothing much and I waited for his hands to start shaking but he sat behind his beard and told me a long story about the time he'd explored the upper tiers of the East Room at the Morgan Library, after regular hours, memorizing the titles on the spines of priceless volumes arrayed just beneath the lavishly muraled ceiling, and I decided not to mention the fact that I'd been with him at the time.

There was a woman on the subway platform, across the tracks. She stood at the wall, in wide trousers and a light sweater, eyes closed, and who does this, on a subway platform, people milling, trains coming and going. I watched her and when my train came I did not board and waited for the tracks to be clear again and resumed watching her, a woman seeming to draw ever inward, so I chose to believe. I wanted her to be the woman I'd seen before, twice, standing on a sidewalk, motionless, eyes closed. The platform began to get crowded and I had to change position to see her. I wondered if she was involved in some kind of cultural tong war, part of a faction in exile working out an interpretation of their role, their mission. This would be the point of the sign, if there was a sign, a message directed to other factions, partisans of another theory, another conviction.

I liked this idea, it made total sense, and I imagined myself leaving the platform, hurrying up the steps and across the street and down the other set of steps and through the turnstile to the other platform to ask her about this, her group, her sect.

But this was a different woman and there was no sign. Of course I'd known this from the start. There was nothing left for me to do but wait for her train to enter the station, people leaving, people boarding. I wanted to be sure she would not be standing there, she would not remain behind, hands folded at her waist, eyes closed, on an empty platform.

• • •

I called and left messages and found myself one day standing across the street from her building, Emma's. A man walked by, dusty boots, a set of keys on a ring dangling from his belt. I checked my keys. Then I crossed the street, entered the lobby and pressed her bell. The inner door was locked of course. I waited and pressed again. I thought of walking to her school and asking someone if I might see Emma Breslow. I spoke the full name inwardly.

Her cellphone was no longer functioning. This was a plunge into prehistory. What was the first thing I would say to her when we spoke, finally?

Compliance and ethics officer.

Then what?

A college in western Connecticut. Not far from the horse farm where we met. You'll come to visit. We'll ride a horse.

I didn't go to her school. I took a long walk on crowded streets and saw four young women with shaved heads. They were a group, they were friends, not flouncing along like runway models dressed for world-weary collapse. Tourists, I thought, northern Europe, and I made a tepid attempt to read meaning into their appearance. But sometimes the street spills over me, too much to absorb, and I have to stop thinking and keep walking.

I called the school and someone said she was on brief leave.

The job was set, start in two weeks, well before the school year begins, time to accompany Ross, time to return, to adjust, and I didn't know how I felt about going back there, the Convergence, that crack in the earth. Here, in the settled measure of days and weeks, there were no arguments to make, no alternatives to propose. I'd accepted the situation, my father's. But I needed to talk to Emma beforehand, tell her everything, finally, father, mother, stepmother, the name change, the numbered levels, all the blood facts that follow me to bed at night.

She called that night, late, speaking in a voice that was all urgency, heavy pressure bearing upon her, word after word. Stak had disappeared. It happened five days ago. She was in Denver now with the boy's father. She'd been there since day two. The police had issued a missing person report. There was a search unit working on the case. They'd confiscated his computer and other devices. The parents were in touch with a private investigator.

Two of them, mother and father, the shared anguish, the mystery of a son who decides to vanish. His father was certain that the boy hadn't been taken and detained by others. There had been signs of some kind of activity beyond Stak's customary stray behavior. That was all. What else could there be? She was exhausted. I spoke briefly, saying what I had to, and asked how I might reach her. She said she'd call again and was gone.

I stood in the bedroom and felt defeated. It was a cheap and selfish feeling, a bitterness of spirit. Rain was hitting the window and I lifted it open and let the cool air enter. Then I looked in the mirror over the bureau and simulated a suicide by gunshot to the head. I did it three more times, working on different faces.

- 7 -

There was a sandstorm wavering across the landscape and the airstrip was unapproachable for a time. Our small plane circled the complex while we waited for a chance to land. From this height the structure itself was a model of shape and form, a wilderness vision, all lines and angles and jutted wings, set securely nowhere.

Ross was in the seat in front of me speaking French with a woman across the narrow aisle. The plane had five seats, we were the only passengers. He and I had been traveling for many hours stretching to days, spending a night in an embassy or consulate somewhere, and I had the feeling that he was drawing things out, not delaying his arrival for the sake of living one more day but simply placing things in perspective.

What things?

Mind and memory, I guess. His decision. Our father-and-son encounter, three-plus decades, all dips and swerves.

This is what long journeys are for. To see what's back behind you, lengthen the view, find the patterns, know the people, consider the significance of one matter or another and then curse yourself or bless yourself or tell yourself, in my father's situation, that you'll have a chance to do it all over again, with variations.

He wore a safari jacket and blue jeans.

The woman had been in her seat when Ross and I boarded this last aircraft. She would be his guide, leading him through the final hours. I listened to them, on and off, caught a phrase here and there, all about procedures and schedules, the detailwork of another day at the office. She may have been in her mid-thirties, wearing a version of the green two-piece garment associated with hospital staff, and her name was Dahlia.

The plane circled lower and the complex appeared to float up out of the earth. All around it the immense fever burn of ash and rock. The sandstorm was out there, more visibly now, dust rising in great dark swelling waves, only upright, rollers breaking vertically, a mile high, two miles, I had no idea, trying to work miles into kilometers, then trying to think of the word, in Arabic, that refers to such phenomena. This is what I do to defend myself against some spectacle of nature. Think of a word.

Haboob, I thought.

When the storm roar reached us and the wind began to bounce the aircraft around, we felt a tangible danger. The woman said something and I asked Ross to interpret.

"The complications of awe," he said.

It sounded French, even in English, and I repeated the phrase and so did he and the plane banked away from the advancing rampart and I began to wonder whether this was a preview in trembling depth of an image I might encounter on one of the screens in one of the empty halls where I would soon be walking.

I wasn't sure whether this was the same room I'd occupied before. Maybe it just looked the same. But I felt different, being here. It was just a room now. I didn't need to study the room and to analyze the plain fact of my presence within it. I set my overnight bag on the bed and did some stretching exercises and squat-jumps in an attempt to shake the long journey from body memory. The room was not an occasion for my theories or abstractions. I did not identify with the room.

Dahlia may have been from this area but I understood that origins were not the point here and that categories in general were not intended to be narrowed or even named.

She took us along a broad corridor where there was an object secured to a granite base. It was a human figure, male, nude, not set within a pod or fashioned from bronze or marble or terra-cotta. I tried to determine the medium, a body posed simply, not a Greek river god or Roman charioteer. One man, headless—he had no head.

She turned to face us, walking backwards, speaking piecemeal French, and Ross translated, wearily.

"This is not a silicone-and-fiberglass replica. Real flesh, human tissue, human being. Body preserved for a limited time by cryoprotectants applied to the skin."

I said, "He has no head."

She said, "What?"

My father said nothing.

There were several other figures, some female, and the bodies were clearly on display, as in a museum corridor, all without heads. I assumed that the brains were in chilled storage and that the headless motif was a reference to pre-classical statuary dug up from ruins.

I thought of the Stenmarks. I hadn't forgotten the twins. This was their idea of postmortem decor and it occurred to me that there was a prediction implied in this exhibit. Human bodies, saturated with advanced preservatives, serving as mainstays in the art markets of the future. Stunted monoliths of once-living flesh placed in the showrooms of auction houses or set in the windows of an elite antiquarian shop along the stylish stretch of Madison Avenue. Or a headless man and woman occupying a corner of a grand suite in the London penthouse owned by a Russian oligarch.

My father's capsule next to Artis was ready. I tried not to think of the mannequins I'd seen on the earlier visit. I wanted to be free of references and relationships. The sight of the bodies confirmed that we were back, Ross and I, and that was enough.

Dahlia led us along an empty hall with doors and walls in matching colors. When we turned the corner there was a surprise, a room with door ajar, and I approached and looked inside. Plain chair, table with several implements evenly spread, small man in a white smock seated on a bench at the far wall.

Seemed ominous to me, a miniature room, bare walls, low ceiling, bench and chair, but it was the setting for nothing more than a haircut and shave. The barber put Ross in the chair and worked quickly, using a thinning scissors and a silent clipper. He and the guide exchanged brief remarks in a language I could not identify. And here was my father's face emerging from the dense hair. The hair was a nest for the face. The shaved face was a sad story, eyes blank, flesh caved beneath the stark cheekbones, jaw turned to mush. Am I seeing too much? The compressed space lends itself to overstatement. Hair shed everywhere, head showing small ruts and lesions. Then the eyebrows, gone so quick I missed the moment.

We had to pause, those around the chair, when my father's hand began to tremble. We stood and watched. We did not move. We maintained a silence that was oddly reverent.

When the shaking stopped, the guide and the barber spoke again, incomprehensibly, and it occurred to me that this was the language I'd been told about, first by Ross and then by the man in the artificial garden, Ben-Ezra, who spoke of a developing language system far more expressive and precise than any of the world's existing forms of discourse.

The barber used traditional razor and foam to finish working the indentations around the mouth and jaw and I listened to Dahlia speak in choppy syllablelike units that were interspersed at times with long-drawn breathless episodes of humdrum monotone. There was a slant of the upper body. There was a thing she did with her left hand.

The barber in halting English told me that the body hair would be removed closer to the time. Then they helped Ross out of the chair and he looked ready. A terrible thought but this is what I saw, a man with nothing left to him but the clothing he wore.

• • •

I walked the halls, a revisitation, each turn of a corner unfurling some hint of memory. Doors and walls. One long hallway sky-dyed, faint vapor trails in hazy grays traced along the upper wall and an edge of the ceiling. I stopped a while to think about something. When did I ever stop in order to think? Time seemed suspended until someone walked by. What sort of someone? I was thinking about the remarks my father had once made concerning the human life span, the time we spend alive, minute to literal minute, birth to death. A period so brief, he said, that we might measure it in seconds. And I wanted to do just that, calculate his life in the context of the interval known as a second, one sixtieth of a minute. What would this tell me? It would be a marker, the last number in an ordered sequence to set alongside the willful tide of his days and nights, who he was and what he'd said and done and undone. A form of memorial emblem maybe, a thing to whisper to him in the final flash of his awareness. But then there was the fact that I didn't know how old he was, how many years, months and days I might convert to a pre-eminent number of seconds.

I decided not to be troubled by this. He had walked out the door, rejecting his wife and son while the kid was doing his homework. *Sine cosine tangent.* These were the mystical words I would associate with the episode from that point on. The moment freed me of any responsibility concerning his particular numbers, date of birth included.

I resumed walking the halls. I was here only provisionally, step by step, assuming the duties of the man, my age and shape, who'd been here before. Then I saw the screen, lower edge, a broad strip, wall to wall, visible beneath the ceiling niche. This was a welcome sight. The serial force of images would overwhelm my sense of floating in time. I needed the outside world, whatever the impact.

I walked to a point within five meters of the place where the screen would lower to the floor. I stood and waited, wondering what sort of event would jump out at me. Event, phenomenon, revelation. Nothing happened. I counted silently to one hundred and the screen remained where it was. I did it again, murmuring the numbers, pausing after each series of ten, and the screen did not lower. I shut my eyes and waited a while longer.

People standing with eyes shut. Was I part of an epidemic of closed eyes?

The emptiness, the hush of the long hall, the painted doors and walls, the knowledge that I was a lone figure, motionless, stranded in a setting that seemed designed for such circumstances—this was beginning to resemble a children's story.

I open my eyes. Nothing happens. A boy's adventures in the void.

I had a clear recollection of the stone room with the huge jeweled skull, the megaskull, adorning one wall. The setting was different this time. A man wearing a dust mask led Ross and me into a location, or a situation, that I recognized as the veer. One of many, I assumed, and there was a moment, a nonmoment, in which time was suspended as we slipped down to one of the numbered levels. Then we followed the man to a boardroom where four others were seated, two on each side of a long table, men and women, all baldheaded and barefaced, wearing loose white garments.

This is what Ross was wearing. He was relatively alert, prompted by a mild stimulant. The guide directed us to facing chairs and then left the room. We tried not to study each other, six of us, and no one had a word to say.

These were individuals self-chosen for the role but immersed nevertheless in the final hours of the one life each had known. I'd welcomed anything that Artis had to say in this situation. These were strangers, this was my father, and a thoughtful silence was a distinct blessing. All the mad fixations submerged for a time.

It was not a long wait. Three men, two women entered, middle-aged, fully dressed, clearly visitors here. They took seats at the far margins of the table. I understood that they were benefactors, private individuals or possibly envoys, one or two of them, from some agency or institute or cabal, as Ross had once explained. Here he was, a benefactor himself, and now a lost shorn figure without a suit or tie or personal database.

Another brief moment, another silence, then the next entrance. Tall somber woman, turtleneck and tight pants, hair bunched afro-style, trace of gray.

I registered these things, I said the words to myself, identified the kind of face and body and apparel. If I failed to do this, would the individual disappear?

She stood at one end of the table, hands on hips, elbows flaring, and she appeared to be speaking into the table itself.

"Sometimes history is single lives in momentary touch."

She let us think about this. I could almost believe that I was meant to raise my hand and give an example.

"We don't need examples," she said, "but here's one anyway. Painfully simplistic. A scientist doing obscure research in a lost corner of a laboratory somewhere. Living on beans and rice. Unable to complete a theory, a formula, a synthesis. Half delirious. Then he attends a conference halfway around the world and shares a lunch and a few ideas with another scientist who has come from a different direction."

We waited.

"What's the result? The result is a new way for us to understand our place in the galaxy."

We waited some more.

"Or what else?" she said. "Or a man with a gun walks out of a crowd toward the leader of a major nation and nothing is ever quite the same."

She looked into the table, thinking.

"Your situation, those few of you on the verge of the journey toward rebirth. You are completely outside the narrative of what we refer to as history. There are no horizons here. We are pledged to an inwardness, a deep probing focus on who and where we are."

She looked at them, one by one, my father and the other four.

"You are about to become, each of you, a single life in touch only with yourself."

Did she make it sound forbidding?

"Others, far greater in number, have come here in failing health in order to die and be prepared for the chamber. You are to be postmarked Zero K. You are the heralds, choosing to enter the portal prematurely. The portal. Not a grand entranceway or flimsy website but a complex of ideas and aspirations and hard-earned realities."

I needed a name for her. I hadn't named anyone on this visit. A name would add dimension to the lithe body, suggest a place of origin, help me identify the circumstances that had brought her here.

"It will not be total darkness and utter silence. You know this. You've been instructed. First you will undergo the biomedical redaction, only a few hours from now. The brain-edit. In time you will re-encounter yourself. Memory, identity, self, on another level. This is the main thrust of our nanotechnology. Are you legally dead, or illegally so, or neither of these? Do you care? You will have a phantom life within the braincase. Floating thought. A passive sort of mental grasp. Ping ping ping. Like a newborn machine."

She took a walk around the table, addressing us from the other end. Never mind giving her a name, I thought. That was last time. I wanted this visit to be over. The determined father in his uterine tube. The aging son in his routine pursuits. The return of Emma Breslow. The position of compliance and ethics officer. Check the wallet, check the keys. The walls, the floor, the furniture.

"If our planet remains a self-sustaining environment, how nice for everyone and how bloody unlikely," she said. "Either way, the subterrane is where the advanced model realizes itself. This is not submission to a set of difficult circumstances. This is simply where the human endeavor has found what it needs. We're living and breathing in a future context, doing it here and now."

I looked across the table at Ross. He was elsewhere, not dreamily adrift but thinking hard, thinking back, trying to see something or understand something.

Maybe I was recalling the same tense moment, two of us in a room and the words spoken by the father.

I'm going with her, he said.

Now, two years later, he was finding his way toward these words.

"That world, the one above," she said, "is being lost to the systems. To the transparent networks that slowly occlude the flow of all those aspects of nature and character that distinguish humans from elevator buttons and doorbells."

I wanted to think about this. *That slowly occlude the flow.* But she kept on talking, looking up from the tabletop to study us in our collective aspect, the earthlings and the shaved otherworlders.

"Those of you who will return to the surface. Haven't you felt it? The loss of autonomy. The sense of being virtualized. The devices you use, the ones you carry everywhere, room to room, minute to minute, inescapably. Do you ever feel unfleshed? All the coded impulses you depend on to guide you. All the sensors in the room that are watching you, listening to you, tracking your habits, measuring your capabilities. All the linked data designed to incorporate you into the megadata. Is there something that makes you uneasy? Do you think about the technovirus, all systems down, global implosion? Or is it more personal? Do you feel steeped in some horrific digital panic that's everywhere and nowhere?"

She needed a name that started with the letter Z.

"Here of course we refine our methods constantly. We are putting our science into the wonder of reanimation. There is no slinking trivia. No drift of applications."

A clipped voice, authoritative, slightly accented, and the tension in her body, the stretched energy. I could call her Zina. Or Zara. The way the capital letter Z dominates a word or name.

The door opened and a man entered. Bruised jeans and a pullover shirt, long pigtail dangling. This was new, the plaited hair, but the man was easily recognizable as one of the Stenmark twins. Which one, and did it matter?

The woman remained at one end of the table, the man took up a position at the other end, informally, with no hint of staged choreography. They did not acknowledge each other.

He made a linked gesture, face and hand, indicating that we have to begin somewhere so let's just see what happens.

"Saint Augustine. Let me tell you what he said. Goes like this."

He paused and closed his eyes, giving the impression that his words belonged to darkness, coming to us out of the centuries.

"'And never can a man be more disastrously in death than when death itself shall be deathless.'"

I thought *what*.

It took him a while to open his eyes. Then he stared over Zara's head into the far wall.

He said, "I won't attempt to set this remark within the meditation on Latin grammar that inspired it. I simply place it before you as a challenge. Something to think about. Something to engage you in your body pod."

The same deadpan Stenmark. But he had clearly aged, face drawn tighter, hands veined a deep blue. I'd given the twins a total of four first names but could not unscramble them now.

"Terror and war, everywhere now, sweeping the surface of our planet," he said. "And what does it all amount to? A grotesque kind of nostalgia. The primitive weapons, the man in the rickshaw wearing a bomb vest. Not a man necessarily, could be a boy or girl or woman. Say the word. *Jinriksha*. Still hand-pulled in certain towns and cities. The small two-wheeled carriage. The small homemade explosive. And on the battlefield, assault rifles of earlier times, old Soviet weapons, old battered tanks. All these attacks and battles and massacres embedded in a twisted reminiscence. The skirmishes in the mud, the holy wars, the bombed-out buildings, entire cities reduced to hundreds of rubbled streets. Hand-to-hand combat that takes us back in time. No petrol, no food or water. Men in jungle packs. Crush the innocent, burn the huts and poison the wells. Relive the history of the bloodline."

Head slanted, hands in pockets.

"And the post-urban terrorist, having abandoned his adopted city or country, what does he contribute? Websites that transmit atavistic horrors. Beheadings out of dreadful folklore. And the fierce interdictions, the centuries' old doctrinal disputes, kill those who belong to the other caliphate. Everywhere, enemies who share histories and memories. It is the patchwork sweep of a world war, unnamed as such.

Or am I crazy? Or am I a babbling fool? Lost wars in remote terrain. Storm the village, kill the men, rape the women, abduct the children. Hundreds dead but guess what—no film or photographs, so what's the point, where's the reaction. And warriorship in brighter light. We see it all the time. Scenes of burning tanks and trucks, soldiers or militiamen in dark hoods standing amid the crushed barbed wire witnessing a conflagration while they pound on a scorched bathtub with hammers and rifle butts and car jacks to send an ancestral drumbeat into the night."

He appeared to be in a state of near seizure, body shaking now, hands whirling.

He said, "What is war? Why talk about war? Our concerns here are wider and deeper. We live every minute in the embrace of our shared belief, the vision of undying mind and body. But their wars have become inescapable. Isn't war the only ripple on the dim surface of human affairs? Or am I brainsick? Isn't there a deficiency out there, a shallow spirit that guides the collective will?"

He said, "Who are they without their wars? These events have become insistent clusters that touch and spread and bring us all into range of a monodrama far larger, worldwide, than we've ever witnessed."

Zara was watching him now and I was watching her. They were clinging to the surface, weren't they, both of them? Earth in all its meanings, third planet from the sun, realm of mortal existence, every definition in between. I didn't want to forget that she needed a surname. I owed her this. Isn't that why I was here, to subvert the dance of transcendence with my tricks and games?

"People on bicycles, the only means of transport for non-combatants in the war zone except for walking, limping or crawling. Running is reserved for the warring factions and for the news photographers who cover the scene, as in earlier world wars. Is there a longing for hand-to-hand, for crush his skull and smoke a cigarette. Car bombings at sacred sites. Rocket launchings by the hundreds. Families living in stinking basements, no lights, no heat. Outside, men are tearing down the bronze statue of the former national hero. A hallowed act, rooted in remembrance, in re-experience. Men in camouflage uniforms spattered with mud. Men in bullet-scarred jeeps. The rebels, the volunteers, the insurgents, the separatists, the activists, the militants, the dissidents. And those who return home to bleak memories and deep depression. A man in a room, where death shall be deathless."

He was deadpan again, faceless, body rocking slightly. Where is his brother? And what is this man's relationship with Zara, although maybe she is Nadya. He has a wife back home, I'd already established this, the brothers married to sisters. I wanted to hear the lively tilt of the twins in their merged commentary. Was the missing twin a sleek nano-body crusted in ice in a lonely pod? Were all pods the same height? And here is Nadya, who stands at the other end of the table. Are they mismatched lovers or total strangers?

Stenmark said, "Apocalypse is inherent in the structure of time and long-range climate and cosmic upheaval. But are we seeing the signs of a self-willed inferno? And are we counting the days before advanced nations, or not so advanced, begin to deploy the most hellish weapons? Isn't it inevitable? All the secret nestings in various parts of the world. Will planned aggressions be nullified by cyberattack? Will the bombs and missiles reach their targets? Are we safe here in our subterrane? And whatever the megatonnage, how will the shock register continent to continent, the blow to world consciousness? How post-Hiroshima and post-Nagasaki? Back to the old shattered cities, to primeval ruin one hundred thousand times more devastating than before. I think of the dead and half-dead and badly injured, nostalgically placed on rickshaws to be pulled across the crushed landscape. Or am I lost in the hazy memory of old film footage?"

I sneaked a look at the bald woman across the table, seated next to Ross. Anticipation, a near joy visible in her face. It didn't matter what the speaker had to say. She was eager to slip out of this life into timeless repose, leaving behind all the shaky complications of body, mind and personal circumstance.

Stenmark appeared to be finished. Hands folded at his midsection, head lowered. In this prayer stance he said something to his colleague. He was speaking the resident language, the unique system of the Convergence, a set of voice sounds and gestures that made me think of dolphins communicating in mid-ocean. She responded with an extended remark that included some head-bobbing, possibly comic in other circumstances but not here, not with Nadya doing the bobbing.

Her accent vanished inside the opaque bubble of whatever she was saying. She left her position and walked along one side of the table, placing her hand on the shaved head of each of the heralds in turn.

"Time is multiple, time is simultaneous. This moment

happens, has happened, will happen," she said. "The language we've developed here will enable you to understand such concepts, those of you who will enter the capsules. You will be the newborns, and over time the language will be instilled."

She turned the corner and swung around to the other end of the table.

"Signs, symbols, gestures and rules. The name of the language will be accessible only to those who speak it."

She placed her hand on my father's head—my father or his representation, the naked icon he would soon become, a dormant in a capsule, waiting for his cyber-resurrection.

Her accent thickened now, maybe because I wanted it to.

"Technology has become a force of nature. We can't control it. It comes blowing over the planet and there's nowhere for us to hide. Except right here, of course, in this dynamic enclave, where we breathe safe air and live outside the range of the combative instincts, the blood desperation so recently detailed for us, on so many levels."

Stenmark walked to the door.

"Ignore the manly directive," he said to us. "It will only get you killed."

Then he was gone. Where to, what next. Nadya looked up and away toward a corner of the room. Her arms were raised now, framing her face, and she spoke in the language of the Convergence. She had a strength of presence. But what was she saying, and to whom? She was a singular figure, self-enclosed, high-collared shirt, fitted trousers. I thought of women in other places, streets and boulevards in major cities, wind blowing, a woman's skirt lifting in the breeze, the way the wind tenses the skirt, giving shape to the legs, making the skirt dip between the legs, revealing knees and thighs. Were these my father's thoughts or mine? The skirt whipping against the legs, a wind so brisk that the woman turns sideways, facing away from the force of it, the skirt dancing up, folding between the thighs.

She was Nadya Hrabal. That was her name.

- 8 -

I was in the chair in my room, waiting for someone to come and take me somewhere else.

I was thinking about the free play of step-by-step and word-for-word that we experience up there, out there, walking and talking under the sky, swabbing on suntan lotion and conceiving children and watching ourselves age in the bathroom mirror, next to the toilet where we evacuate and the shower where we purify.

Now here I am, in a habitat, a controlled environment where days and nights are interchangeable, where the inhabitants speak an occult language and where I am forced to wear a wristband that contains a disk that reports my whereabouts to those who watch and listen.

Except that I wasn't wearing a wristband, was I? This visit was different. A deathwatch. The son permitted to accompany his father into the depths, beyond the allowable levels.

I slept for a time in the chair and when I woke up my mother was present in the room. Madeline or her aura. How strange, I thought, that she might find me here, now in particular, in the wake of the woeful choice that Ross has made, her husband for a time. I wanted to sink into the moment. My mother. How ill-suited these two words were to this huge cratered enclosure, where people maintained a studied blankness about their nationality, their past, their families, their names. Madeline in our living room with her avatar of personal technology, the mute button on the TV remote. Here she is, a breath, an emanation.

I used to follow her along the stately aisles of the enormous local pharmacy, a boy in his neo-pubescence, his budhood, reading the labels on boxes and tubes of medication. Sometimes I sneaked open a container to read the printed insert, eager to sample the impacted jargon of warnings, precautions, adverse reactions, contraindications.

"Time to stop mousing around," she said.

I'd never felt more human than I did when my mother lay in bed, dying. This was not the frailty of a man who is said to be "only human," subject to a weakness or a vulnerability. This was a wave of sadness and loss that made me understand that I was a man expanded by grief. There were memories, everywhere, unsummoned. There were images, visions, voices and how a woman's last breath gives expression to her son's constrained humanity. Here was the neighbor with the cane, motionless, ever so, in the doorway, and here was my mother, an arm's length away, a touch away, in stillness.

Madeline using her thumbnail to gouge price stickers off the items she'd purchased, a determined act of vengeance against whatever was out there doing these things to us. Madeline standing in place, eyes closed, rolling her arms up and around, again and again, a form of relaxation. Madeline watching the traffic channel, forever it seemed, as the cars crossed the screen soundlessly, passing out of her view and back into the lives of the drivers and passengers.

My mother was ordinary in her own way, free-souled, my place of safe return.

The escort was a nondescript man who seemed less a human being than a life-form. He led me through the halls and then pointed to the door of the food unit and went away.

The food tasted like medicated sustenance and I was trying to think my way through it, to defeat it mentally, when the Monk walked in. I hadn't thought of the Monk in some time but hadn't forgotten him either. Was he here only when I was here? He wore a plain brown robe, full-length, and was barefoot. This made sense but I didn't know why or how. He sat at the facing table, seeing only what was in his plate.

"We've been here before, you and I, and here we are again," I said.

I looked at him openly. I mentioned his account of the journey he'd made to the holy mountain in Tibet. Then I watched him eat, his head nearly in the plate. I mentioned our visit to the hospice, he and I—the safehold. I surprised myself by recalling that word. I spoke the word twice. He ate and then I ate but I kept watching him, long hands, condensed look. He was wearing his last meal on his robe. Did it fall off his fork or did he vomit it up?

He said, "I've outlasted my memory."

He looked older and the sense he carried with him of nowhereness was more pronounced than ever and in fact this is where we were. Nowhere. I watched him nearly consume his fork with the food that was on it.

"But you still visit those who are waiting to die and to be taken down. Their emotional and spiritual needs. And I wonder if you speak the language. Do you speak the language being spoken here?"

"My entire body rejects it."

This was encouraging.

"I speak only Uzbek now."

I didn't know what to say to that. So I said, "Uzbekistan."

He was finished eating, the plate scraped clean, and I wanted to say something before he left the unit. Anything at all. Tell him my name. He was the Monk, who was I? But I had to pause. For a long bare moment I could not think of my name. He stood, pushed back the chair and took a step toward the door. A moment between being no one and someone.

Then I said, "My name is Jeffrey Lockhart."

This was not a remark he could assimilate.

So I said, "What do you do when you're not eating or sleeping or talking to people about their spiritual well-being?"

"I walk the halls," he said.

Back to the room, to the shaved space.

All the zones, the sectors, the divisions that I hadn't seen. Computer centers, commissaries, shelters for attacks or natural disasters, the central command area. Were there recreational facilities? Libraries, movies, chess tournaments, soccer matches? How many numbers in the numbered levels?

• • •

He was naked on a slab, not a hair on his body. It was hard to connect the life and times of my father to this remote semblance. Had I ever thought of the human body and what a spectacle it is, the elemental force of it, my father's body, stripped of everything that might mark it as an individual life. It was a thing fallen into anonymity, all the normal responses dimming now. I did not turn away. I felt obliged to look. I wanted to be contemplative. And at some far point in my wired mind, I may have known a kind of weak redress, the satisfaction of the wronged boy.

He was alive, hovering at some level of anesthetic calm, and he said something, or maybe something was said, a word or two seeming to rise out of the body spontaneously.

A woman in a smock and surgical mask stood on the other side of Ross. I looked at her, more or less for approval, and then leaned toward the body.

"*Gesso on linen.*"

I think this is what I heard, then other slurred fragments that were not comprehensible. The sunken face and body. The man's depressed dick. The rest of him simply limbs, projecting parts.

I nodded at the sound of the words and exchanged a brief look with the woman and then nodded again. I knew only that *gesso* was a term used in art, a surface or medium. Gesso on linen.

I was allowed a moment alone, which I spent staring into space, and then others came to prepare Ross for his long slow sabbatical in the capsule.

• • •

I was led to a room in which all four walls were covered with a continuous painted image of the room itself. There were only three pieces of furniture, two chairs and a low table, all depicted from several angles. I remained standing, turning my head and then my body to scan the mural. The fact of four plane surfaces being a likeness of themselves as well as background for three objects of spatial extent struck me as a subject worthy of some deep method of inquiry, phenomenology maybe, but I wasn't equal to the challenge.

A woman eventually entered, smallish, brisk in a suede jacket and knit trousers. She had eyes that seemed to stream light and this is what made me realize that she was the woman in the surgical mask who'd stood across from me during the crude viewing of the body.

She said, "You prefer to stand."

"Yes."

She considered this, then took a seat at the table. There was a silence. No one entered with tea and cookies on a tray.

She said, "There were many discussions, Ross and Artis and I. We are born without choosing to be. Should we have to die in the same manner? The resources he placed at our disposal were of crucial importance."

What else did I see? She wore a scarf that was striking in design and I decided that she was fifty-five years old, of local origin, more or less, and a figure of some authority.

"After Artis entered the chamber I spent time with your father in New York and in Maine. He was more generous than ever. Although a man transformed. Of course you know this. Reduced to near shreds by the loss. Isn't it a human glory to refuse to accept a certain fate? What is it that we want here? Only life. Let it happen. Give us breath."

I understood that she was speaking to me out of respect for my father. He had asked, she was complying.

"We have language to guide us out of dire times. We are able to think and speak about what can conceivably happen in time to come. Why not follow our words bodily into the future tense? If we tell ourselves forthrightly that consciousness will persist, that cryopreservatives will continue to nourish the body, it is the first awakening toward the blessed state. We are here to make it happen, not simply to will it, or crawl toward it, but to place the endeavor in full dimension."

Her fingers vibrated when she spoke. I was slightly wary. Here was a woman coiled in thought, instant by instant, determined to make things happen.

"I'm done with theories and arguments," I said. "Ross and I, we talked and shouted our way through all the levels."

"He said that you never called him Dad. I said, How un-American. He tried to laugh but could not quite manage."

In my bland shirt and pants I could imagine myself drifting into the wall painting and going unnoticed, a dusky figure in a corner of the room.

"Human life is an accidental fusion of tiny particles of organic matter floating in the cosmic dust. Life continuance is less accidental. It utilizes what we've learned in the thousands of years of our humanity. Not so random, not so chancy, but not unnatural."

"Tell me about your scarf," I said.

"Goat cashmere from Inner Mongolia."

It was increasingly clear that she was a significant member of this undertaking. If the Stenmark twins were the creative core, the jokester visionaries, did this woman generate the income, set the direction? Was she one of the individuals who originated the idea of the Convergence, setting it in this harsh geography, beyond the limits of believability and law. A financier, a philosopher, a scientist who has broadened her role here. What was her particular experience? I would not inquire. And I would not ask her name or create one for her. This was my version of progress. Time to go home.

But she said there was one final site that Ross wanted me to visit. She led me to a veer, she and I with two escorts, and we went farther into the numbered levels than I'd gone before. How did I know this? I felt it, bone-deep, although no evidence of lapsed time or ostensible distance was apparent.

I was taken to an alcove and fitted with a breathing apparatus and a protective suit that resembled spacewear. It was not cumbersome and it allowed me to immerse myself in the unreal state of the occasion.

The woman said, "It's only natural that we've endured some setbacks, a few stalled plans, an occasional mishap. There have been instances of hopes frustrated."

She was looking out at me from her respirator.

"There are measures in effect that will maintain your father's support although not at previous levels. There's a foundation and an administrator and a number of inhibiting limits and safeguards and time factors."

"You have support from other directions."

"Of course, always. But what Ross did for us was a turning point. His unwavering faith, his worldwide resources."

"You've had defections perhaps."

"His willingness to be a participant in the most telling manner."

We were led slowly along a narrow passageway.

On one wall there was a cracked clay tablet set horizontally and bearing a tightly compressed line of numbers, letters, square roots, cube roots, plus and minus signs, and there were parentheses, infinities and other symbols with an equal sign in the midst of it all, an indication of logical or mathematical equality.

I didn't know what the equation was meant to signify and I had no intention of asking. Then I thought of the Convergence, the name itself, the word itself. Two distinct forces approaching a point of intersection. The merger, breath to breath, of end and beginning. Could the equation on the plaque be a scientific expression of what happens to a single human body when the forces of death and life join?

"Where is he now?"

"He's in the process of cooldown. Or soon will be," she said. "You are the son. Of course he made me to understand that you have reservations about this concept, this location as well. Skepticism is a virtue on certain occasions, although often a shallow one. But he never characterized you as a man with a closed mind."

I wasn't only his son, I was *the* son, the survivor, the heir apparent.

We encountered access tubes and airlocks and entered

the cryostorage section. We were without escorts now and we went along a walkway that was slightly elevated. Soon an open area came into view and seconds later I saw what was in it.

There were rows of human bodies in gleaming pods and I had to stop walking to absorb what I was seeing. There were lines, files, long columns of naked men and women in frozen suspension. She waited for me and we approached slowly, at a height that provided clear perspective.

All pods faced in the same direction, dozens, then hundreds, and our path took us through the middle of these structured ranks. The bodies were arranged across an enormous floor space, people of various skin color, uniformly positioned, eyes closed, arms crossed on chest, legs pressed tight, no sign of excess flesh.

I recalled the three body pods that Ross and I had looked at on my earlier visit. Those were humans entrapped, enfeebled, individual lives stranded in some border region of a wishful future.

Here, there were no lives to think about or imagine. This was pure spectacle, a single entity, the bodies regal in their cryonic bearing. It was a form of visionary art, it was body art with broad implications.

The only life that came to mind belonged to Artis. I thought of Artis in her fieldwork, the time of mud trenches and crawl spaces, the objects dug up, earth-crusted tools and weapons, incised limestone fragments. And was there something nearly prehistoric about the artifacts ranged before me now? Archaeology for a future age.

I waited for the woman with the Mongolian scarf to tell me that here was a civilization designed to be reborn one day long after the catastrophic collapse of everything on the surface. But we walked and paused and walked again, in silence.

If this is what my father wanted me to see, then it was my corresponding duty to feel a twinge of awe and gratitude. And I did. Here was science awash in irrepressible fantasy. I could not stifle my admiration.

I thought finally of lavishly choreographed dance routines from Hollywood musicals of many decades past, dancers synchronized in the manner of a marching army. Here, there were no cuts or dissolves or soundtracks, no motion at all, but I kept on looking.

In time I followed the woman along a corridor that had murals of ravaged landscapes, on and on, scenes meant to be prophetic, a doubled landscape, each wall repeating the facing wall—disfigured hills, valleys and meadows. I looked left and right and left again, testing one wall against the other. The paintings had a kind of spiderwork finesse, a delicacy that intensified the ruin.

We came finally to an arched doorway that led into a small narrow room, stone-walled, in faint light. She gestured and I entered and after several steps forward I had to stop.

At the far wall there were two streamlined casings, taller than those I'd just seen. One was empty, the other held the body of a woman. There was nothing else in the room. I did not approach for a closer look. It seemed required of me to maintain an intervening space.

The woman was Artis. Who else would it be? But it took a while before I was able to absorb the image, the reality, attach her name to it, let the moment seep into me. I took a few steps forward, finally, noting that her body stance did not match the pose of all the others in their pods.

Her body seemed lit from within. She stood erect, on her toes, shaved head tilted upward, eyes closed, breasts firm. It was an idealized human, encased, but it was also Artis. Her arms were at her sides, fingers cusped at thighs, legs parted slightly.

It was a beautiful sight. It was the human body as a model of creation. I believed this. It was a body in this instance that would not age. And it was Artis, here, alone, who carried the themes of this entire complex into some measure of respect.

I thought to share my feelings, if only by look or gesture, a simple nod of the head, but when I turned to find the woman who'd led me here, she was gone.

The empty capsule would belong to Ross of course. His body shape would be restored, face toned, his brain (in local lore) geared to function at some damped level of identity. How could this man and woman have known, years ago, that they would reside in such an environment, on this sub-planet, in this isolated room, naked and absolute, more or less immortal.

I looked for a time, then turned to find an escort standing in the doorway, younger person, genderless.

But I wasn't ready to leave. I remained, eyes closed, thinking, remembering. Artis and her story of counting drops of water on a shower curtain. Here, the things to count, internally, will be endless. *Forevermore*. Her word. The savor of that word. I opened my eyes and looked a while longer, the son, the stepson, the privileged witness.

Artis belonged here, Ross did not.

• • •

I followed the escort into the veer and then out along a series of halls where there was a closed door every twenty meters or so. We came to an intersection and the escort pointed down an empty hallway. It was all simple sentences, subject, predicate, object, things narrowing down, and I was alone now, my body shrinking into the long expanse.

Then a wrinkle, a crease in the smooth surface, and I saw the screen at the end of the hall just as it began to lower, and here I am again, waiting for something to happen.

The first figures appeared even before the screen had fully unfurled.

Troops in black-and-white come striding out of the mist.

It's a formidable image, undercut nearly at once by the crushed body of a soldier in camouflage gear sprawled in the front seat of a wrecked vehicle.

Stray dogs roaming the streets of an abandoned urban district. A minaret visible at the edge of the screen.

Troops in snowfall, crouched together, ten men spooning some slop from wooden bowls.

An aerial shot of white military trucks passing through a barren landscape. Maybe a drone image, I thought. Trying to sound informed, if only to myself.

I realized there was a soundtrack. Faint noises, engines revving, remote gunfire, voices barely audible.

Two armed men seated in the bed of a pickup truck, each with a cigarette dangling from his mouth.

Men in robes and headscarves throwing stones at a target that remains offscreen.

Half a dozen troops poised within a ruined battlement, looking over the parapet, rifle butts protruding from the wall notches, and one soldier wears a comic-strip facemask, brightly colored, long pink face with green eyebrows, rouged cheeks and a leering red mouth. Everything else is black-and-white.

I did not have to ask myself what the purpose was, the meaning behind all this, the mindset. It was Stenmark. It was here because. The visual equivalent, more or less, of his address to the group in the boardroom.

The boardroom. When was that? Who exactly was in the group? Stenmark's world war. The man passionate, trembling at times.

Men in black walking single-file, each with a long sword, sunup, ritual murder, black head to foot, a chill discipline marking their stride.

Soldiers asleep in a bunker, stacks of sandbags.

Exodus: masses of people carrying whatever possessions they can manage, clothing, floor lamps, carpets, dogs. Flames rising across the screen behind them.

It takes me a while to notice that the soundtrack has become pure sound. A prolonged signal that rejects any trace of expressive intent.

Riot police tossing stun grenades at people retreating across a broad promenade.

Two elderly people on bicycles in devastated terrain. In time they ride alongside a column of tanks in a snowy field, a single limp body visible in a ditch.

Bodies: slaughtered men in a jungle clearing, vultures stepping among the corpses.

It was awful and I watched. I began to think of others

watching, other screens, other halls, level after level throughout the entire complex.

Children outside a minivan, waiting to enter, black smoke hanging still in the distance, one child looking back that way, the others turned toward the camera, faces blank.

Hand-to-hand, six or seven men with knives and bayonets, some in camo jackets, concentrated bloodletting, up close, a tall man staggered, ready to fall, the others thrusting into the instant of stop-action.

Another drone image, ruined town, ghost town, small figures scavenging among the rubble.

A soldier's unshaved face, the raw warrior breed, black knit cap, cigarette jutting from his mouth.

A cleric in rapid stride, Orthodox priest, canonical garments, his cape, his cassock, people marching behind him, others joining, folding into the picture, fists raised.

Facedown corpse on a potholed road, bomb debris everywhere.

The halls are jammed with people watching the screens. All of them thinking my thoughts.

Another comic-strip facemask, a cartoon facemask, a soldier among others, formed up, rifle held across upper body, his white face, purple nose, red lips curled in a sardonic sneer.

A woman in a chador, seen from the rear, stepping out of a car and walking head-down into a crowded square where a few people notice and watch and then begin to scatter, camera pulling back, then the blast, purely visual, seeming to rip the screen apart and shred the air around us. All those watching.

Mourners at graveside, some with automatic weapons strapped over their shoulders, the same black smoke seen earlier, a long way off, not climbing or spreading but utterly, eerily still, resembling a painted backdrop.

A small child with a funny hat squatting bare-ass to crap in the snow.

Then there is a pause and the steady keening noise of the soundtrack fades away. The screen fills with a numb gray sky and the camera slowly levels and the first impressive image is repeated.

Troops come striding out of the mist.

But this time the shot is prolonged and the men keep coming and there are wounded among them, limping figures, bloodied faces, a few men helmeted, most wearing black knit caps.

Sound resumes, realistic now, explosions somewhere, aircraft flying low, and the men begin to advance more warily, weapons held tight to bodies. They move past a mound of burning tires into city streets, buildings collapsed, wreckage everywhere. I watch them walking over shattered stonework and there are isolated shouts soon overwhelmed by the concentrated discharge of weapons.

It looks and sounds like traditional war, men in arms, and I recall the warped nostalgia that Stenmark had talked about, all the world wars embedded in these images, a soldier with a cigarette in his mouth, a soldier asleep in his bunker, a bearded soldier with a bandaged head.

Sounds of local gunfire and the men take cover, searching out the source, firing back, and the soundtrack flows into the action, loud, close, voices calling, and I have to step back from the screen even as the camera becomes more intimately involved, creeping along the terrain for close-ups of men's faces, young and not so young, fingers gripping triggers, bodies edged against the frame of a ruined structure. It's quick and clear and magnified, a sense of something impending, and all I'm able to do is watch and listen, a sudden clutter of sound and image, the camera sways and jitters and then finds a man standing in the hulk of a wrecked car, rifle sweeping the area. He fires several times, upper body flinching in rhythm. He ducks down and waits. We all wait. The camera scans the area and it is empty debris and light rain and then the single figure is back in sight, kneeling on the driver's seat and firing once out of the shattered side window. Periods of near silence and the camera remains angled on the crouched man, who wears a headband, no helmet, and then the firing resumes from various quarters and the picture jumps and the man is hit. This is what I think I see. The camera loses him and catches only traces of muddled background. The noise becomes intense, rapid firing, a voice repeating the same word, and then he is back, wandering out into the open, without his rifle, camera steadying, and he is hit again and goes to his knees and I'm reciting these words to myself as I watch. He is hit again and goes to his knees and there is a distinct image of the figure, khaki field jacket, jeans and boots, spiky hair, he is three times life size, here, above me, shot and bleeding, stain spreading across his chest, young man, eyes shut, surpassingly real.

It was Emma's son. It was Stak.

He topples forward and the camera spins away and that's who it was, the son, the boy. Battle tanks approaching now and I need to see him again because even though there is no doubt, it happened too fast, it was not enough. A dozen tanks in lazy array rolling over sandbag barriers and I stand here waiting. Why would they show it again? But I have to wait, I need to see it. The tanks move along a road that bears a sign with Cyrillic and Roman characters. *Konstantinovka*. There is a crude drawing of a skull above the name.

Stak in Ukraine, a self-defense group, a volunteer battalion. What else could it be? I keep looking and waiting. Did the recruiters know his age or even his name? He's a native son come home. Birth name, acquired name, nickname. All I know is Stak and maybe this is all there is to know, the kid who became a country of one.

I have to stay until the screen goes dark. I have to wait and see. And if they send an escort for me, the escort will have to wait. And if Stak doesn't reappear, then let the picture fade, the sound die, the screen roll up, the entire hall go dark. The other halls empty out, an orderly flow of people, but this hall goes dark and I stand here with my eyes shut. All the times I've done this before, stand in a dark room, motionless, eyes shut, weird kid and grown man, was I making my way toward a space such as this, long cold empty hall, doors and walls in matching colors, dead silence, shadow streaming toward me.

Once the dark is total, I will simply stand and wait, trying hard to think of nothing.

- 9 -

I see a taxi parked three or four feet from the sidewalk and then a man in the gutter on his knees, shoes off, set behind him, and he is bowing, head to the pavement, and it takes me a moment to understand that he is the driver of the taxi and that the direction is Mecca, he is bowing toward Mecca.

On weekends, now and then, I stay in a guest room in my father's townhouse, with kitchen privileges. The young man who deals with these matters, one of the corporate effigies, discusses details in the contemporary pattern of declarative sentences that slither gradually upward into questions.

Sometimes I think I go to museums just to hear the languages spoken by visitors to the galleries. Once I followed a man and woman from the limestone grave markers in fourth-century B.C. Cyprus all the way to Arms and Armor, waiting for them to resume talking to each other so I could identify the language, or try to, or make a dumb guess. The thought of approaching them to ask, politely, was outside my range.

I sit before a screen in a cubicle of frosted plexiglass marked Compliance and Ethics Officer. I've adapted well here, not just in terms of my day-to-day disposition but in the context of the methods I've developed to perform the requisite duties and conform to the indigenous language.

Beggar in wheelchair, dressed normally, clean shaven, no stained paper cup, gloved hand thrust into the street swarm.

There's the wide-ranging dynamic of my father's corporate career and there's the endland of the Convergence and I tell myself that I'm not hiding inside a life that's a reaction to this, or a retaliation for this. Then, again, I stand forever in the shadow of Ross and Artis and it's not their resonant lives that haunt me but their manner of dying.

When I ask myself why I requested an occasional overnight visit to the townhouse, I think at once of the building where Emma lives, in this general area, or where she used to live, and I take frequent walks in the neighborhood, expecting to see nothing, learn nothing, but feeling an immanence, the way in which a painful loss yields a shadow presence, and in this case, on her street, I sense a possibility that I haven't even tried to understand.

In my local market I never forget to check the expiration dates on bottles and cartons. I reach into the display of objects, of packaged goods, and lift an item from the last rank because that's where the freshest sliced bread is placed, or milk, or cereal.

Women tall and taller. I look for the woman in a formal pose standing on a street corner with or without a sign in an obscure alphabet. What is there to see that I haven't seen, what lesson is there to be learned from a still figure in the midst of crowds? In her case it may be an issue of impending threat. Individuals have always done this, haven't they? I think of it as medieval, a foreboding of some kind. She is telling us to be ready.

Sometimes it takes an entire morning to outlive a dream, to outwake a dream. But I haven't been able to recall a single faint instant of dreamtime since my return. Stak is the waking dream, the boy soldier looming onscreen, about to come crashing down on top of me.

• • •

I go walking, looking, and it is stalled and moaning traffic and it is foreign money soaring into the penthouse towers that outclimb the zoning laws.

I like the idea of working in school surroundings, knowing that at some point the idea will dissolve into the details. A van arrives very early Monday, already carrying two employees who live in Manhattan, and we travel to a small community in Connecticut where the college is located, a modest campus, students of middling promise. We remain until Thursday afternoon, when we are driven back to the city, and it's interesting how we find new ways, the three of us, to talk about nothing.

The long soft life is what I feel I'm settling into and the only question is how deadly it will turn out to be.

But do I believe this or am I searching for effect, a way to balance the ease of my everydayness?

I enter the room with the monochrome paintings, recalling the final words that Ross managed to speak. *Gesso on linen*. I try to absolve the term of its meaning and to think of it as a fragment of some beautiful lost language, unspoken for a thousand years. The paintings in the room are oil on canvas but I tell myself that I will visit museums and galleries and search for paintings designated gesso on linen.

●　●　●

I walk for hours, dodging a splotch of dogshit now and then.

Emma and I, lovers upon a time. My smartphone remains at my hip because she is out there somewhere, in the digital wilderness, and the ringtone, rarely heard, is her implied voice, an instant away.

I eat sliced bread because I can make it last longer by refrigerating it, which doesn't work with Greek or Italian or French bread. I eat thick crusty bread in restaurants, dining mostly alone by choice.

All of this matters even if it's not supposed to matter. The bread we eat. It makes me wonder who my forebears were, but only briefly.

I know I'm supposed to resume the smoking habit. Everything that has happened drives me in that direction, theoretically. But I don't feel reduced by my abstinence, as I did in the past. The craving is gone and maybe this is what reduces me.

There is an elegant lamp hanging from the ceiling in the guest room of the townhouse and I turn it on and turn it off and every time I do this, inescapably, I find myself thinking of the term *pendant light*.

• • •

On the street, going nowhere special, I check my wallet and keys, I check the zipper on my pants to make sure that it's fastened securely from beltline to crotch or vice versa.

The relief is not commensurate with the fear. It lasts a limited time. You worry for days and then months and finally the son arrives and he is safe and you forget how you could not concentrate on another subject or situation or circumstance in all that time because now he's here, so let's eat dinner. Except that he's not here, is he? He's somewhere near a road sign reading Konstantinovka, in Ukraine, his place of birth and death.

Languages, sirens all the time, beggar in a bundled mass, man or woman, awake or asleep, alive or dead, hard to tell even when I approach and drop a dollar in the dented plastic cup.

Two blocks farther on I tell myself that I should have said something, determined something, and then I change the subject before it gets too complicated.

I sit in my cubicle in the administrative offices at the college and cross things off lists. I don't erase the items, I click the strikethrough check box and run a line through each item on the screen that needs to be eliminated. Lines and items. Over time the lines through the items mark my progress in a readily visible way. The instant of the strikethrough is the best part, with childlike appeal.

I think of the few moments we spent looking at ourselves in the mirror, Emma and I, and it was first person plural, a blended set of images. And then my sad damning failure to tell her who I was, to narrate the histories of Madeline and Ross, and Ross and Artis, and the still-life future of father and stepmother in cryonic suspension.

I waited too long.

I'd wanted her to see me in an isolated setting, outside the forces that made me.

Then I recall the taxi driver kneeling in the gutter slime, turned toward Mecca, and I try to reconcile the firm placement of his world into the scatterlife of this one.

Sometimes I think of the room, the scant roomscape, wall, floor, door, bed, a monosyllabic image, all but abstract, and I try to see myself sitting in the chair and that's all there is, highly detailed, this thing and that thing and the man in the chair, waiting for his escort to knock on the door.

The restoration, the scaffolding, the building facade hidden behind great white sweeps of protective sheathing. The bearded man who stands beneath the scaffold shouting at everyone who walks past and it's not words or phrases we hear but sheer sound, part of the noise of taxis, trucks and buses except that it issues from a human.

I think of Artis in the capsule and try to imagine, against my firm belief, that she is able to experience a minimal consciousness. I think of her in a state of virgin solitude. No stimulus, no human activity to incite response, barest trace of memory. Then I try to imagine an inner monologue, hers, self-generated, possibly nonstop, the open prose of a third-person voice that is also her voice, a form of chant in a single low tone.

On public elevators I direct a blind gaze precisely nowhere, knowing that I'm in a sealed box alone with others and that none of us is willing to offer a face open to inspection.

I'm standing at a bus stop when Emma calls. She tells me what happened to Stak, using the least number of words. She tells me that she has quit her job at the school and given up her apartment here and will stay with the boy's father and I can't remember whether they were divorced or separated, not that it matters. The bus comes and goes and we talk a while longer, quietly, in the manner of near strangers, and then we assure each other that we'll talk again.

I don't tell her that I saw it happen.

- 10 -

This was a crosstown bus, west to east, a man and woman seated near the driver, a woman and boy at the rear of the bus. I found my place, midway, looking nowhere in particular, mind blank or nearly so, until I began to notice a glow, a tide of light.

Seconds later the streets were charged with the day's dying light and the bus seemed the carrier of this radiant moment. I looked at the shimmer on the back of my hands. I looked and then listened, startled by a human wail, and I swerved from my position to see the boy on his feet, facing the rear window. We were in midtown, with a clear view west, and he was pointing and wailing at the flaring sun, which was balanced with uncanny precision between rows of high-rise buildings. It was a striking thing to see, in our urban huddle, the power of it, the great round ruddy mass, and I knew that there was a natural phenomenon, here in Manhattan, once or twice a year, in which the sun's rays align with the local street grid.

I didn't know what this event was called but I was seeing it now and so was the boy, whose urgent cries were suited to the occasion, and the boy himself, thick-bodied, an oversized head, swallowed up in the vision.

Then there is Ross, once again, in his office, the lurking image of my father telling me that everybody wants to own the end of the world.

Is this what the boy was seeing? I left my seat and went to stand nearby. His hands were curled at his chest, half fists, soft and trembling. His mother sat quietly, watching with him. The boy bounced slightly in accord with the cries and they were unceasing and also exhilarating, they were prelinguistic grunts. I hated to think that he was impaired in some way, macrocephalic, mentally deficient, but these howls of awe were far more suitable than words.

The full solar disk, bleeding into the streets, lighting up the towers to either side of us, and I told myself that the boy was not seeing the sky collapse upon us but was finding the purest astonishment in the intimate touch of earth and sun.

I went back to my seat and faced forward. I didn't need heaven's light. I had the boy's cries of wonder.

About the Author

Don DeLillo is the author of fifteen previous novels, one story collection and three stage plays. His novels include *White Noise*, *Libra*, *Underworld* and *Falling Man*, and he has won many honors in this country and abroad, most recently the National Book Foundation's Medal for Distinguished Contribution to American Letters.